NOT SO SWEET TOFFEE

BY TOFFEE KEENOR-LEACH

I dedicate this book to the old man and the old woman who keep me supplied with prawns

'It is a truth universally acknowledged, that people in possession of good taste and intelligence, must be in want of a cat.'

KITTY QUOTES

In ancient times cats were worshipped as gods; they have not forgotten this. *Terry Pratchett*

My cat is not insane; she's just a really good actress. *P.C. Cast*

The way to get on with a cat is to treat it as an equal – or even better, as the superior it knows itself to be. *Elizabeth Peters*

Cats can work out mathematically the exact place to sit that will cause most inconvenience. *Pam Brown*

Dogs come when they're called; cats take a message and get back to you later. *Mary Bly*

My cats inspire me daily. They inspire me to get a dog! *Greg Curtis*

No amount of time can erase the memory of a good cat, and no amount of masking tape can ever totally remove his fur from your couch. *Leo Dworken*

After scolding one's cat one looks into its face and is seized by the ugly suspicion that it understood every word. And has filed it for reference. *Charlotte Gray*

Cats' hearing apparatus is built to allow the hooman voice to easily go in one ear and out the other. *Stephen Baker*

When my cats aren't happy, I'm not happy. Not because I care about their mood but because I know they're just sitting there thinking up ways to get even. *Percy Bysshe Shelley*

A cat isn't fussy – just so long as you remember he likes his milk in the shallow, rose-patterned saucer and his fish on the blue plate. From which he will take it, and eat it off the floor. *Arthur Bridges*

There is, incidentally, no way of talking about cats that enables one to come off as a sane person. *Dan Greenberg*

I love cats because I enjoy my home; and little by little, they become its visible soul. *Jan Cocteau*

THE WORLD ACCORDING TO TOFFEE

Let me introduce myself. I am Toffee. I didn't name myself. If I had I would be called something like Killer Queen or Amazonian Warrior. But, no. Those people I so generously allow to share my home decided to call me Toffee. WHAT IS WRONG WITH THEM? I am sooo not sweet.

I adopted the old man and the old woman when I was a kitten. They don't think they're old but in cat years they must be at least twelfty eleventeen. I have trained them into the Ways of Toffee but they still have a few annoying habits which I try to overlook as they keep me well supplied with my favourite food. PRAWNS. Droooooool.

They keep out of my fur for much of the time as they are at work. I'm not sure what they do all day but they complain about it a lot. The old man sets off for something he calls a workshop and the old woman works part-time in an office.

Her primary function seems to be to make lots of cups of tea and sample various kinds of cake that her colleagues bring to work to celebrate anniversaries, births of babies, the death of Henry The Eighth, their dog being de-wormed, that kind of thing. On her days off her primary function also seems to be making cups of tea and eating cake. In fact if there were an Olympic event for drinking tea and eating cake, she'd be a gold medallist.

Some may call me spoilt but I prefer to think superior treatment is my due. I demand high standards from my hoomans and most of the time that's what I get. Unfortunately their care occasionally falls below the quality demanded. But I forgive them. They are only hooman after all.

JANUARY

January 1

Hello, dear reader. Due to popular demand I have decided to write a journal to keep you abreast of The Fascinating Life and Times of Toffee.

It can't have escaped your notice that today is January 1. I'm not making any New Year resolutions. Last year I made four and broke them all by January 2. The one about not helping myself to food in the kitchen fell at the first hurdle. There were prawns. Nuff said. I was unable to give up cardboard boxes, sleeping until noon or shredding inappropriate objects.

I made a resolution for the old man and the old woman but they are so terminally dim it never got off the ground. I wanted them to start buying me gourmet cat food in those little tin foil trays like you see the posh boy cats eating on the tellybox. This was a non-starter. Despite my staring pointedly at the telly-box and meowing every time posh boy cat appeared they took not notice, except one time when the old woman said, 'I think Toffee's got a bit of thing for that cat. She reacts every time he's on TV.' I'm not reacting to HIM, you daft old bat, but to what's he's eating. As I said, dim.

A year later, apart from special occasions, I'm still getting bog standard pouches and tins. But I haven't given up the hope that one day I will be like that pedigree puss who dips his paw into premium diced steak and smugly licks it off. Gissa job, I can do that.

So my only resolution this year is to share my life with you.

If I can be bothered.

January 2

The old woman's New Year fitness regime has begun. So far it has consisted of watching a fitness DVD from the sofa and conditioning her arms by repeated lifting of biscuit to mouth. My New Year regime is going well, thank you for asking. I've decided to up my level of sleeping and today managed a record of 22 hours and 35 minutes.

Result!

January 3

Not much to report today. I had a hot date with a plumped up cushion that needed unplumping. Took me eight hours.

January 4

The old man and the old woman rushed around like blue-arsed flies this morning. They did something called 'over-sleeping'. Apparently *someone* knocked the alarm clock to the floor in the middle of the night and it didn't go off at the appointed hour.

They glared at me in between running about finding shoes and bags. I sat by my empty food bowl and gave them a very pointed look indeed.

'It would serve you right if you had nothing to eat all day, Toffee,' said the old man through a mouthful of toast.

Yesss, I notice YOU managed to find time to stuff your ravening maw with YOUR breakfast.

He eventually poured some chicken chunks in gravy into my bowl before rushing out the door, the old woman in hot pursuit.

What is wrong with these people?

January 5

Dear Old Woman, thank you for that 'educational' toy you gave me today. Let's see how 'educational' it is after being dropped onto a concrete path from a bedroom window.

January 6

It's Twelfth Night so the old woman took down the Christmas decorations. I helped.

I like Christmas decorations although they don't taste as good as you might think - and they seem to be very shod-

9

dily made as they fall apart at the slightest provocation. They should be more robust, in my opinion.

I don't know what the old woman would have done without my help. I heard her telling the old man, 'It took hours, thanks to this one,' and pointed at me.

I can only surmise that without my assistance it would have taken days.

January 7

The old man was reading the newspaper and came up with the fact that a hummingbird eats its own weight in food every day.

He glanced at me as I was chewing on a few treats and said to the old woman, 'Toffee thinks she's a hummingbird,' and they both laughed.

Noodleheads.

January 8

The old woman visited a friend who has recently acquired two kittens. She came home with lots of photographs. There were kittens playing, kittens being stroked, kittens climbing up curtains, kittens clinging to her shoulder. In one picture the pair of them dangled from her lobes like two giant ear-rings.

I sincerely hope the old man and the old woman aren't contemplating adopting any kittens. I don't think I could cope with that level of cuteness.

January 9

In order to increase the sum of feline knowledge, I have over several months investigated the effects of gravity on random objects. Here are the results of my experiments:

Coffee mug: Breaks. Effect: Liquid content spreads and stains pale rug. Secondary effect: The old woman rushes to get the carpet cleaner and several damp cloths and towels.

Jar of jam: Shatters. Effect: Floor becomes sticky. Very sticky. Secondary effect: If anyone walks through it they will leave jammy footprints all over the floor, duvet, cushions, furniture. Saying nothing...

Newspaper: Falls apart. Effect: The old man bundles it back together while swearing. Quite loudly. Secondary effect: The old man starts reading an article and becomes very confused because he's got the pages in the wrong order.

Glass bowl: Breaks spectacularly. Effect: The old woman becomes upset because it was a gift from Aunt Maud. Secondary effect: The old man does a fist pump when she isn't looking because he's always hated it.

Pillow: Falls to the floor and looks very inviting. Too inviting. Effect: Zzzzzzzz. Secondary effect: Zzzzzzzz.

I'm thinking of changing my name to Einstein and offering my services to the Department of Science at the University of Oxford.

January 10

I have liberated a bowl of prawns from the bourgeois clutches of a capitalist lackey.

She wasn't best pleased.

January 11

'Curiosity killed the cat, Toffee,' the old man told me.

Thanks for that but why didn't you tell me BEFORE I got my head stuck in the sleeve of the old woman's coat.

Long story. Don't ask.

January 12

What a day I've had. It was freezing cold but I braved the outside to do what a cat without a litter tray in the house has to do. I'd just finishing my morning constitutional when I had a run-in with the stupid cat next door. When he moved in he told me his name was Rajah and looked down his nose at me. Today was taunting me with a half-eaten chunk of beef which he had no doubt stolen. He has the morals of an alley cat.

I was about to make a dash to take it off him and return it (ahem) when a sparrow pooped on me from a great height. Rajah (Ooo, I'm So Grand I'm Part Persian) sat there chewing on the beef and laughing at me between mouthfuls. Moron. It took ages to clean the disgusting stuff from my fur.

I went indoors to eat some salmon in jelly to take the taste of bird poo out of my mouth but my food bowl was empty. I was forced to drink water to swill out the vile substance.

I tried to forget all my troubles by having a nap but I was kept awake by the incessant caterwauling of Rajah (Ooo, I'm So Grand I'm Part Persian) slugging it out with several other cats in the neighbourhood. It's astonishing the effect dead cow has on the feline population.

By the time the old man and the old woman came home from work, I was tired, hungry and in a SERIOUSLY BAD MOOD.

Then the pair of them sat down to watch a programme about dogs on the tellybox. Dogs! Have they none of the finer sensibilities?

They decided on an early night and by the time I decided to retire, the bedroom door was firmly shut and no amount of scratching and meowing persuaded them to open it.

I can now hear them snoring.

I have been abandoned.

January 13

Excuse me. It's time you groomed me with that lovely bristly thing. I have a minuscule speck of dirt on my rump I am finding difficult to get rid of.

Jump to it.

January 14

As I sit here by myself with only my favourite toy Mr Fluffy Bum to keep me company, I ruminate on all the things that on occasion make my life less than perfect.

Sub-standard food. Don't try to fob me off with food from a can or pouch you opened ten minutes ago. It is stale.

Not sharing food. Whatever you have on your plate is of interest to me. Let me have a taste or I will keep annoying you until you do. I may not normally eat cheese, sauces, eggs or pancakes, but they suddenly taste delicious if they come from your plate.

Being ignored. There is no excuse for pushing me away, no matter how gently. Excuses I will not accept: urgent deadlines, need to get the housework done, sudden medical emergency, a bathroom crisis or a meteor falling on the house.

Belly rubs. Belly rubs per se do not make me angry. I will roll on my back to signal that I would not be displeased by a gentle scratch of this region. However, be aware that if you rub my belly for one nano second too long, I will ATTACK. You have been warned.

Restriction of sleeping places. I get angry when bedroom doors and laptop lids are banged shut as I approach. Make sure there is always a newspaper laid out on the sofa - so much the better if you are in the middle of reading it and you've just put it down to answer the phone. I get angry when you will not allow me to sleep on your head, or right up under your chin so you are immobilised and cannot watch the tellybox, or on your feet or legs so you cannot move. If you stretch your legs out on the sofa, you must expect me to make use of them.

Any little moving thing. Flies, spiders, mice, birds - and those stupid little toys on sticks you shake in front of me can be annoying, or not. It depends what mood I'm in. To humour you I might play with that toy you seem so ridiculously proud to have bought but be aware that I *will* shred it when you're not looking. Which leads me to…

Expensive cat-related objects: It's plain stupid to spend money on objects when you could be buying juicy prawns or things that will make my life so much more comfortable. I have a rule: the more expensive the toy, the less interest I will show in it. Hence my preoccupation with cardboard boxes.

Loud noises. It may sound like a faint rustle to you but to a sensitive being like me, it is worse than standing next to a pneumatic drill without ear defenders. I will run off like a wildebeest being chased by a lion and hide in the smallest space I can find until tempted out by plump fresh prawns.

Other things that make me angry include: being outdoors when it's raining, being indoors when it's sunny, too much affection, too little affection, Christmas baubles, ornaments on shelves, tassels, other cats, dogs, strangers, the postman, string, people knocking on the door, being woken up, being stroked (sometimes), not being stroked (sometimes), ribbons, bells and whistles.

As you can see, I'm quite laid-back on the whole.

January 15

I decided I wanted to see a 'waterfall'. Quick trip to the bathroom where I pushed the lever with my paw. Sorry you were sitting on the toilet at the time, old woman, but did you have to make such a fuss?

January 16

This morning I was really hungry. The old man piled up my bowl with rabbit in gravy and it disappeared in double quick time. The old woman saw the empty bowl and assumed I hadn't been fed, so she gave me a whole lot more which I soon cleared up. The old man returned to the kitchen and said, 'You must be hungry, girl, here have some coley in jelly,' and proceeded to open another pouch.

In the garden I spotted a takeaway carton which upon investigation revealed two half-eaten burgers. Waste not, want not.

Mrs Hartley from number 46 saw me with my head in the carton. 'Goodness, Toffee, Are you hungry?' She popped back across the road to her house and returned with some cold lamb. Don't mind if I do!

I slept all day and then in the evening it was more rabbit in gravy and a saucer of cat milk. That's milk FOR cats, not FROM cats – thought I'd better make that clear. The old man and the old woman had fish for tea, which they kindly shared. Later I had a snack of cheese pinched off the old man's plate and cream left over from the old woman's pudding.

I am now stretched out on the sofa cuddled up to Mr Fluffy Bum contemplating these wise words from Miss Piggy, 'Never eat more than you can lift.'

January 17

Today I made a startling discovery. Hooman beings cannot

twitch their ears. This fact came to light when the old man and the old woman were asleep. I flicked the old man's ears with my paws a couple of times but they remained resolutely solid, although his lobes did jiggle a bit. I am now outside the bedroom and the door is firmly shut.

I do not think these two occurrences are related.

January 18

It's been an interesting day. The old woman decided to convert the box room into a cat play area after reading on the internet that cats need stimulation. If I needed stimulation I'd go and pick a fight with Rajah.

She spent hours lugging around furniture to clear a space. She tacked a scratching board to the wall and nailed up wide shelves accessible by a ladder. There was a big basket filled with toys. Cupboard drawers were pulled out and lined with cushions. Cardboard boxes and cardboard tubes were scattered around.

She lifted me up and plonked me in a box.

'There, Toffee, this is your very own room. What do you think?'

It's OK but I prefer to be downstairs.

January 19

Cat play area remains empty despite the old woman's best efforts to lure me in. I briefly paid a visit to eat the prawns she had placed in a bowl and put into one of the boxes but then I wandered downstairs again.

January 20

Play area empty.

January 21

Brief check of play area to see if it contained prawns. It did not.

January 22

Play area reverts to box room.

January 23

I came across three mice in the garden today. Despite information to the contrary, none of them was blind. They scattered in three directions and disappeared before I could make up my mind which one to chase.

Devious.

January 24

I'm writing my diary early today as I might not have time to write later. I've eaten breakfast, removed the butter from the old man and the old woman's toast, had my morning constitutional in the garden, swiped at a low-flying bird and licked all my important little places. I have circled the cushion on the sofa to make a big soft depression. Now I'm exhausted. Need to sleep.

A short 12-hour nap should do it.

January 25

The old woman spent part of the morning clearing up a bag of sugar I had 'accidentally' (ahem) knocked to the floor. In the afternoon I demanded her attention on head, chin, back and belly rubbing duties. This evening she washed up my bowls and scrubbed the plastic mat they sit on before resuming her function as my chief entertainments officer. This involved playing peekaboo with a cushion.

'I used to be a career woman,' she moaned. 'How did I get to be Mad Cat Woman?'

It's nothing to complain about, old woman. Cat Woman is a noble and prestigious profession.

January 26

The old man and the old woman take far too much notice of advertisements for my liking. Hence a loft full of discarded exercise equipment (like a mini trampoline used once), electrical products (why buy some strange electrical gadget for peeling apples when there is a handy peeler in the drawer?) and things that sounded like a good idea at the time (who needs a heart-shaped fried egg for their breakfast? Seriously. Who?)

I don't care about what they buy for themselves but the other day when they were watching some programme about animals, an advert came on for dog and cat toothbrushes. They looked at each other. They looked at me. The old woman pried open my lips to look at my teeth. The old man peered into my mouth. I snapped my mouth shut on the old woman's fingers. The old man fetched a sticking plaster.

'I don't think we'll bother,' said the old woman.

Good move.

January 27

The old woman isn't talking to the old man. She bought an expensive jar of face cream and was showing him the list of all the wonderful things it was going to do to her fizzog.

He whispered to me, 'I think that ship has sailed.'

The whisper was a tad loud... and you couldn't fail to hear the slammed door.

The house is still shaking.

January 28

I'm off now for a spot of environmental interaction*.

*Looking out the window.

January 29

Mrs Hartley popped in for a cup of tea this morning. She's nice enough - always bends down to rub my ears which I quite like. The old woman likes her too but often complains she can't get rid of her.

The old woman made tea in a pot and got out the best cups with saucers. Very posh. It's usually a tea bag plonked into her *I Love Cats* mug. Out came the biscuits too. I looked meaningfully into my empty bowl and gave a little meow but it had no effect. Nothing for me at this little tea party, I notice.

You know me, I'm not one to make a fuss. In any case I had just finished my breakfast. I had snaffled a few prawns the old woman was defrosting for later and drank a bowl of cat milk. I felt as full as a tick. Still, an acknowledgment that I was part of the proceedings would have been polite.

I settled down on a dining table chair while the old woman and Mrs Hartley rabbited on about everything, from her at number 16, who's no better than she ought to be, apparently, whatever that means, and the price of fish during which my ears pricked up briefly. But it was just a throwaway remark - 'what does that have to do with the price of fish?' - which had nothing to do with fish at all. I'll never understand hoomans.

I closed my eyes as they droned on and was soon chasing mice in the Land of Nod.

I woke up an hour later and Mrs Hartley was still chattering away. I noticed the old woman's eyes kept straying to the clock and she'd started to nod politely. Mrs Hartley had outstayed her welcome. The old woman kept starting sentences with things like: 'Well, it's time I...' And 'Gosh, is that the...' but was never allowed to finish them.

Time for Toffee to save the day, I think. I stretched, got down from the chair and wandered over to Mrs Hartley. I sniffed her trousers. They smelled of week-old cabbage and cheap polyester. If anyone rubbed against her I'm sure sparks would fly. Just as an experiment I did just that. No sparks. Disappointing.

She bent down to rub my ears. I took the opportunity to bite her hand and throw up tuna in jelly mixed with milk and prawns all over her sensible shoes.

She screamed, clutched her hand and stared down horror-struck at her shoes. The old woman leapt to her feet apologising profusely while getting out a cloth for the shoes and antiseptic to dab on Mrs Hartley's hand. What a fuss. I hadn't even broken skin.

Mrs Hartley waved her away. 'No, no. It's fine. I was going anyway,' she said, and ran out the door.

The old woman stared crossly at me. 'Toffee, what on earth did you think you were doing?'

Well, there's gratitude for you. I turned my back on her and stalked out through the open door into the garden.

January 30

Breakfast was late for the second time this week. So I ate three spiders, some fluff and a piece of dried up pork crackling which I found last week under the sofa and was saving for just such an occasion - and puked them up in the old man and the old woman's shoes.

They must learn the lesson.

Incidentally, this week I have so far eaten the equivalent of a large packet of prawns. You will be interested to hear that despite warnings to the contrary from the old man and old woman I have not turned into a prawn.

They are such bullshitters sometimes.

January 31

Rajah was hunting in MY garden this morning. The cheek of it. I hissed at him and he ran off, leaping over the fence into his own garden. His owner was calling him and I found out that his real name is Percy. I nearly died laughing. Percy!

FEBRUARY

February 1

The old man and the old woman went to bed early. They have to be up at the crack of dawn to visit the old woman's niece Violet who has just had a baby. They seem very excited about Little Person. They have been cooing over a video Violet sent them and looking at lots of photographs of Little Person on Facebook. Is it acceptable to comment, 'Yikes!'? Possibly not.

I know beauty is in the eye of the beholder but really. There's obviously something very wrong with Little Person. It is already bald and toothless and seems unable to talk - at least I never heard any words, just an eerie piercing cry. It's like experiencing a horror movie at first hand.

I fear there may be jackals in their garden.

February 2

The old man and the old woman came home full of delight after meeting Little Person. It appears it's got a name, Zeke. Eek would have been more appropriate in my opinion.

He was SO cute, SO bonny, SO sweet, SO lovely.

I can only take SO much.

February 3

When I head-butt you, you must drop everything and pay me attention. I don't care if you are reading, watching the tellybox, on your laptop or on your phone. It's the law.

The old woman got the message when I knocked the mobile out of her hand while she was wittering on to one of her daft friends. Look, no one is the slightest bit interested in Tom Hardy's photo shoot in his scanties. He's not even a cat.

Stroke me. Stroke me now.

February 4

I have trained the old man and the old woman to buy me decent cat food by simply refusing to eat anything else. But today there was trouble in paradise.

They usually do the shopping together but because the old woman was again visiting Violet and Little Person, the chore was left to the old man. Unfortunately, not to put too fine a point on it, he's not the sharpest knife in the drawer. He set off for the supermarket bearing a list as long as a toilet roll.

When he got home and plonked the carrier bags on the kitchen floor, I nosed around looking for my Plumptious Pieces In Gravy. Instead, all I found was the supermarket's OWN BRAND. Yes, I know, you're shocked. OWN BRAND.

When the old woman inspected the shopping later she said, 'Toffee won't eat that.'

The old man was annoyed. 'What do you mean, she won't eat that? She's a cat for God's sake, not Gordon bloody Ramsay.'

The old woman shook her head while the old man spooned some of the solidified mess into my bowl. I sniffed it. Then, tail held high, turned and stalked away.

'Told you,' said the old woman with a hint of triumph in her voice.

'She'll eat it when she's hungry,' said the old man.

Of course, I didn't. I popped next door and pinched some tasty chicken out of Rajah/Percy's bowl. He caught me, which resulted in a bit of a contretemps - but some ruffled fur is a small price to pay for a bowl of gourmet nibbles.

I went home and sat on the sofa, panting pathetically.

'Look what you've done!' yelled the old woman. 'She's already looking really ill. That cheap stuff is POISON to a cat like Toffee.'

'Don't be ridiculous,' said the old man, 'She hasn't even eaten any yet.'

'No, but ... No, but ... She's sniffed it and the poison could have wafted up her nostrils and into her blood stream.'

The old man snorted in derision. 'I'm not even going to dignify that with a response.'

By late evening the gloop was still in the bowl. I put Stage 2 of my plan into operation. With both of them watching, I dragged myself to the bowl, took two mouthfuls and promptly threw up.

You'll be happy to hear there is no need for Stage 3, which is just as well as I'm not sure what Stage 3 entails. The old man threw up his hands in surrender, got in the car and drove off to the 24-hour supermarket for some Plumptious Pieces In Gravy.

Throwing up on demand is a skill all cats should master.

February 5

I need to be on high alert at all times. If it were not for me the old man and the old woman would have been kidnapped by aliens long ago.

I have to be ready for the fray so I keep my claws as honed as a fishmonger's filleting knife. I sharpen where I can - the furniture, the stairs, doors and on the hooman head.

Not all of these - in fact none of them - seem to be acceptable for some reason. Hoomans provide us with objects called 'scratching posts'. These are handy if they are right beside you when you get the urge to hone, but cats are not going to walk any distance to find one, 'any distance' being further than six inches.

Today I learned that of all my claw-honing techniques the one involving the hooman head is the least acceptable.

Go figure.

February 6

Exercising hard today to build up my muscles. Not to keep fit but to drag that joint of beef off the table.

Hungry.

February 7

I spotted that twit Rajah/Percy strutting about my garden. The cheek of it. There he was leaving his stinky scent everywhere.

I ran out and chased him off. He scooted to the top of the fence and we proceeded to trade insults.

'That's right, run scaredy cat!' I yowled.

'Yeah, cos I'm soooo scared of a ginger ball of fluff!'

'You will be if you get down off that fence. So come on, PERCY, do your worst.'

He stared at me.

'Don't call me that,' he growled.

'Not my fault you call yourself Rajah when your real name is PERCY.

'Percy, Mr Percy Plain, Percy the Prat,' I taunted him.

He was furious and jumped back down on my side of the fence.

I ran as fast as I could back through my cat flap. But I'm not a coward. Oh no. I was sure I heard someone calling me, even though the old man and the old woman are both at work.

Yes I did.

February 8

I was asleep on the sofa when the old man left for work this morning. I was asleep on the sofa when he came home from work this evening.

I opened one eye as he flopped down beside me. He rubbed my ears, 'Have you been sleeping all day long?' he asked, in a rather accusing tone of voice.

I was going to get up and flounce out the room with my tail swishing. But I couldn't be bothered and went back to sleep.

February 9

The old man dangled a bird on a string in front of me. *Toy* bird, unfortunately. It swung backwards and forwards. I stared at it briefly before shutting my eyes. Then I felt the darn thing banging into my face. I opened my eyes, crossed my paws and stared meaningfully at the old man. 'OK, Toffee, I get the message,' he said and put the bird down.

I've trained him well.

February 10

Where's my toy bird. I want my toy bird. Give me my toy bird NOW!

February 11

Today I had a brainwave which I need to communicate to all cats. To prevent blood from staining your soft cushion, put the dead mouse under the duvet cover in the master bedroom.

February 12

I felt quite energetic today. I started in the sitting-room where I pulled all the cushions off the sofa onto the floor with the intention of sleeping on them later. Then a pesky fly caught my eye, buzzing about at the top of the bookcase. I scaled the bookcase as quick as a rat up a drainpipe and leapt on the fly. I missed, lost my footing and fell to the floor, dragging books with me as I went.

One was called *The Art of Housework*.

Ironic.

All that effort made me hungry so I skittered into the kitchen for a snack. But I kept thinking about those cushions. I tried to drag my bowl into the sitting-room so I could eat and rest at the same time. Not a total success. Chicken in gravy spilled onto the floor as I went. I retrieved some of it later (via my mouth) but I left quite a few chunks scattered about and accidentally ground some into the floor.

After a short nap, I went out into the garden to survey my domain. Rajah/Percy was strolling about as if he owned the place. I attacked and chased him through a muddy puddle and back over the fence.

Time to go in and clean myself up after my heroic exertions. Mmm, I hadn't realised my feet were *quite* so muddy. I decided to clean them off in the comfort of my own bed. So I climbed the stairs to the master bedroom, which I kindly allow the old man and the old woman to share, hopped up onto the duvet and commenced cleaning. Eventually, I was very clean. Not so the duvet, alas.

I heard the key in the front door so ran downstairs to greet the old man and the old woman. The old woman walked from kitchen to sitting-room, tutting as she went.

She said to the old man: 'What does she do when we're not here? Hold kick-boxing parties?'

And she hasn't seen the bedroom yet.

February 13

I upset the old man by luring him to scratch my belly and then attacking his hand. 'I'm going to swap you for gerbil,' he told me.

The man should get help. He's clearly insane.

February 14

Today is something called Valentine's Day. It's when hoomans get all lovey-dovey and give each other cards and presents.

I got a card from 'A Secret Admirer' and some special cat treats. Not much of a secret as I saw the old woman writing the card and wrapping the present.

The old man got a card and some electronic gizmo he'd been dropping hints about for weeks. He was delighted and handed over a present to the old woman. She ripped the paper off excitedly. Then her face fell.

'A garlic press and an electric tin opener? You got me a garlic press and a tin opener for Valentine's Day?'

Then *his* face fell. 'But you said you wanted a garlic press and the tin opener is *electric*,' he said.

She flung the presents at him and stalked out of the room saying: 'Don't come near me. Don't come anywhere near me.'

He's gone out now...with his wallet.

Later, the house is full of flowers, chocolates and the smell of very expensive perfume.

February 15

Potato crisps. What's all that about? The old man and the old woman sit on the sofa with a pile of snacks in front of them, grumbling about how hard it is to lose weight. They dip their chubby fingers into bags labelled Salt and Vinegar, Cheese and

Onion and Sweet Chilli. Today they had a bag of Roast Chicken flavour crisps. Oh, I thought, that's more like it.

I politely asked the old woman for a taste, by clawing at her hand and meowing. She begrudgingly gave me one. I pounced on it and took a bite. Yeuh...help me! It tasted like a greasy sock. If any part of a chicken had ever got near it, it was its poop. I stalked off to wash my mouth out with my own rabbit pate.

February 16

Feeling soppy. Long cuddle on the sofa with the old man.

February 17

I wish the old man and the old woman were intelligent enough to understand cat. Meow, meow, meow, meow in the kitchen means, 'Feed me now!' Meow, meow, meow, meow in the sitting-room means, 'You're not paying me enough attention.' Meow, meow, meow, meow in the middle of the night means, 'I'm wide awake. Why aren't you?'

Context is all.

February 18

Today I overindulged in woodlice and spiders. I threw them all up in the sitting-room while the old man and the old woman were watching the tellybox, The old woman shouted: 'Eee-ewwww!' and the old man yelled: 'For God's sake, Toffee!'

I thought they'd be pleased I was getting enough roughage.

February 19

A man came to mend the washing-machine. I was temporarily banned from the utility room. Strange, I didn't realise there was any situation which couldn't be enhanced by my scintillating personality.

February 20

I'm keeping away from the old man. He's just finished a huge, very hot, takeaway curry. The old woman and I have taken refuge in the kitchen to escape the devastating effects of noxious gases emitting from both ends of his body.

'I don't know why he insists on eating hot curry. He knows it doesn't agree with him,' she said to me.

She had the good sense to order butter chicken which, although a little spicy for my taste, was palatable once she had sucked the sauce off the chunks and nibbled away the outside.

Later: The old man has been informed that he must sleep in the spare bedroom tonight. At the moment he's flat out on the sofa, snoring.

His breath smells like a spice factory next to an abattoir.

February 21

When will the old man and the old woman learn that anything left lying about is a cat toy? They are not too bright and continue to place desirable objects around the house in the mistaken belief they will not be played with.

Which is why this evening the old man was none too pleased at the state of his phone. What a fuss. It may have a few teeth marks on it but it still works.

Today the old man learned a valuable lesson.

And I learned quite a few new words.

February 22

Today the old man came home with a new phone. He spent all evening trying to get it to work. He was fiddling around with something called a SIM card. I pushed my head up close to see if there was anything I could do to help but he didn't want my assistance. Strange.

He shouted to the old woman: 'Get this darn cat away from me before she wrecks another phone!'

What? I was only trying to help.

Ungrateful wretch.

February 23

Got told off for scratching a door. Speak to the paw, lady, speak to the paw.

February 24

The old woman has downloaded a new app. It's supposed to turn photographs into works of art in the style of various painters like Rembrandt and Vermeer. She's been on the computer searching for suitable subjects. I was shocked to discover she was looking loads of photographs of ME.

She spent all day transmogrifying perfectly good pictures of feline perfection into hideous fuzzy depictions,

Words fail me. Jackson Pollock? Jackson Pillock, more like. Pointillism? Should be What's The Pointillism. As for Pick Ass-hole, or whatever his name was, was he BLIND? How did my head end up sticking out of my ass? As for the one called Old Master. I'M A GIRL AND I AM NOT OLD.

What a lummox she is.

February 25

This evening the old man said to me: 'Did you hear about the cat who swallowed a ball of wool, Toffee?'

I was worried. I hoped that poor cat was OK. Swallowing a small piece of wool could be dangerous, but a whole ball? I feared for her. The old man didn't looked worried at all. In fact he was laughing.

'She had mittens!'

'Your jokes are pathetic,' said the old woman.

Joke? No joke to the poor cat who swallowed the wool. I'm glad there was a positive outcome, what with the wool turning into mittens. But it could all have ended tragically.

So, old man, I think that laughter was completely inappropriate, don't you?

February 26

There's this theatre in Hollywood where big celebrities leave their handprints in cement. This bit of news interested me not a jot, until the old man added that some animals had left their prints, including that supposedly 'cute' dog from the film The Artist. I don't know what all the fuss was about. He's just some scruffy oik who runs about a lot. Anyone can do that. It's not exactly Oscar material, is it?

Now here's the thing. Why has no one asked me to leave MY paw prints? It must be because the theatre is in America and I live in Great Britain. I expect whoever organises these things is concerned about the long journey.

That can be the only explanation.

February 27

Message to self: I must not chew up vast quantities of tissues and spit them down the lavatory.

February 28

Well done, old woman, you've just broken the world record for taking the longest time to park a car. I was watching her from the comfort of my sleeping spot under the weigela bush. She was trying to park in the road because the old man's car and the window cleaner's van were parked in the drive.

You've never seen anything like it - over and back, over and back, over and back. She's just stepped out of the car looking so proud because she's managed to park it a foot from the pavement at a crazy angle.

Never mind, only a short walk to the pavement and with a bit of luck the next car that drives past will manage to avoid taking off your wing mirror.

MARCH

March 1

I caught the old woman looking at a website article called How To Train Your Cat. After half an hour of studying she announced, 'I'm going to train Toffee to sit on command.' The old man laughed ... and laughed ... and laughed. He must have been watching a comedy programme on the tellybox.

She went to the fridge to fetch some prawns. Ah, things were looking up.

She moved the prawn around above my head, keeping it just out of reach.

'What the hell are you doing?' asked the old man. 'Toffee will have your eye out in a minute.'

Damn you. You have warned her of my next move.

'No. This is what you are *supposed* to do. If Toffee sits down, I will give her a prawn.

'Sit, Toffee.'

Why didn't you say so? I sat down. I got the prawn.

The old woman was triumphant. 'Well done, Toffee. Good girl, Toffee. What a little star. Who's a clever pussycat? You are! Yes, you are!'

All right, old woman, that's enough of that. I haven't discovered a cure for cancer.

March 2

Today the training continued. Out came the bag of prawns - yay! The old woman wafted one around in front of my nose.

'Sit, Toffee,' I sat down. I got the prawn and all the fuzzy wuzzy praise again. Frankly, I could have done without the ballyhoo. The prawn was reward enough.

After four or five prawns, she said, 'Sit, Toffee.' I stared at her meaningfully. She had forgotten to hold up the prawn.

'Sit, Toffee.' Pause. 'Sit, Toffee. Toffee, sit.' Pause. 'Sit, Toffee.' The old man began to snigger.

I stared at her again and meowed loudly to tell her YOU'VE FORGOTTEN THE DAMN PRAWN. Then it dawned on me. She wanted me to act like a performing seal and do the little party trick just for the *promise* of a prawn.

Bugger that for a game of soldiers. I leapt at the bag of prawns, accidentally scratching her hand (sorry, collateral damage) and raced off with them into the garden, the old man's laughs echoing in my ear.

Funny, the old woman hasn't tried to 'train' me since.

March 3

The old man and the old woman got out their supermarket 'bags for life' to set off for the weekly shop.

Bags for life? It would be more accurate if they were called Bags for Cake, Crisps, Wine and Beer. Get a grip, Tesco.

March 4

Both the old man and the old woman are at work today. I am alone.

I sat on the kitchen windowsill staring out into the back garden. Not much to see out there apart from some straggly plants, a scrappy lawn and shed. But then my ennui was broken by the sight of Rajah/Percy strutting across the lawn. He looks as if God had intended to make a proper cat but had then changed His mind at the last minute and had accidentally crossed him with a stoat.

I was going to chase him off but I couldn't be bothered.

Still alone. Sometimes I think Mr Fluffy Bum is my only friend.

March 5

The old woman bought a flat-pack cupboard for the bedroom. Assembling flat-pack items holds no fears for this family. The old man reckons he's a dab hand at making sense of assorted planks, screws and dowels. He is not. Not least because the first thing he does is throw away the instructions. All he needs, it seems, is an electric screwdriver, a steel ruler and a six-pack of beer.

So the old woman decided to take on the project herself. Three hours and much blood, sweat and tears later the cupboard sits in the corner looking, I have to admit, very smart.

But the old woman doesn't seem delighted. She is eyeing up the cupboard and sighing.

'What do you think, Toffee? It's a bit plain.'

She thinks a while longer.

'I might try a few stencils or I could paint it.'

It's my turn to sigh. The old woman is to DIY what the Kardashians are to shy and retiring.

March 6

I need you to rub between my ears. NOW. You need to soothe that huge brain of mine before it explodes under the strain of all my intelligence.

March 7

Neither the old man nor the old woman are exactly life's young dream any more, if they ever were. I know they look at me and wonder how I can retain my svelte physique and devastating good looks without seeming to lift a paw.

But they don't see what goes on behind the scenes. True, I sleep for 18 hours a day but those six hours I am awake, I am like a well-oiled machine, ready to spring into life at any second. I am honed, toned and ready for action.

Let me tell you about my fitness regime.

Firstly, diet. I eat 99.9% protein. Unlike the old woman, I never stuff my face with cakes or biscuits and unlike the old man, I consume no beer with its empty calories. They could learn a lot from me. I expend calories in order to consume calories. Some of those spiders and mice are pretty nippy, let me tell you. If the old man and the old woman had to harvest the wheat and hops before they could have a beer, or chase down a bullock or two before they could eat a steak, they wouldn't be worrying about their weight.

I build exercise into my day. For example, there is an ornament on top of the bookcase. Jumping and climbing to get to it so I can send it flying to the ground keeps me fit. I do deep stretches every time I wake from a slumber.

The old man and the old woman think I am having a 'funny five minutes' when I suddenly start chasing a ball around the house. No, I am practising my eye to paw co-ordination and doing my cardio work-out. Similarly, they smile when I leap into the air for no apparent reason. Silly people, it's all part of the Toffee Keep Fit Regimen.

They laugh when I come hurtling through the cat flap at a rate of knots and may ask, 'Did something frighten you in the garden, Toffee?' I comb my whiskers and try to appear nonchalant because I am a brave cat and the barking dog across the road doesn't scare me a bit. Oh no. What I am doing, old man and woman, is speed training. Obvs.

So that is why there is not an ounce of fat on me. You hoomans would do well to follow my example.

Not the hurtling through the cat flap bit, you'd get stuck.

March 8

I got so tired thinking about exercise yesterday that I slept all day.

March 9

Do you remember that cupboard the old woman bought for the bedroom? She had a go at 'improving' it today.

She found an article on the internet about 'distressing' furniture which is when, for some reason I am unable to fathom, people take a perfectly good piece of new furniture and turn into something looking old and knocked about.

Out came the sandpaper, a chisel, a sponge and two colours of paint.

Half a day later and she had certainly achieved her aim of distressing it.

The old man came home from work and went up to the bedroom to fetch a book.

There came a yell. 'What the hell have you done to that cupboard?'

The old woman huffed and puffed.

'You know NOTHING!' she yelled back. 'It's been distressed. It's all the fashion now.'

The old man came to the top of the stairs and shouted down, 'Distressed? It's bloody mortified!'

The cupboard is now in the spare bedroom and the old man and the old woman are sitting at opposite ends of the sofa, not talking to each other.

March 10

The old man read out a story from his newspaper about two cats who had been left a house and $250,000 in their owner's will.

Look, I know I can be slightly grumpy at times but I don't wish the old man and the old woman any harm. I might puke up in their shoes and jump on to their heads from the bookcase but I would never go so far as to leave one of my toys in a lethal position at the top of the stairs.

Anyway, I'd have to wait for them to accrue a bit more money than they have at the moment. They'd be hard-pressed to leave me 25 quid, let alone $250,000.

Not only that, I don't fancy living a life without a couple of hooman pets. They come in handy for back rubs, occasional treats, providing a warm place to lie on and regular feeding.

But not all cats are as friendly and laid-back as I am and I can see a few who might want to take the opportunity to live a pampered existence for the rest of their lives. Their hoomans should be afraid. Very afraid. But as for my pair, they're safe.

For now.

March 11

The old man and the old woman were sitting at the computer, cooing over a couple of tabby kittens. But what do I care?

Jealous? Me? Don't be silly. I am The Special One. Why would I be jealous? It's a ridiculous notion. I have never been jealous in my life. I am Toffee Cat - the Top Cat, the Boss Cat, The Toff.

I don't care if you ogle other cats. Why would I? I know you would never replace me. I am Number One in your affections. Numero Uno.

Why have you both gone out? What time is it? What time are you coming home? I'm lonely. I want a cuddle ...

Oh, here they come. Do they have a box of kittens? Can I hear plaintive meowing? No, they are both wearing coats, sturdy shoes and red faces. I think they have been for a walk.

Told you there was nothing to worry about.

March 12

The old man said to the old woman, 'I'm going to buy a parrot.'

She stared at him. 'A parrot? I don't want a parrot. What would Toffee think?'

Toffee is thinking, 'Ah, flying dinner.'

'No, hear me out. I buy a parrot, hide Toffee away from visitors who know we have a cat and teach the parrot to say, "Meow, they've turned me into a parrot!" What do you think?'

The old woman said, 'I think you're a fool.'

I think he's a cast iron clot.

March 13

The old man dropped half a sausage roll on the floor, swooped down, picked it up and ate it. I didn't see anything wrong with that but the old woman went ballistic.

'That's disgusting!' she screamed. 'What about all those germs! You'll make yourself ill!' On and on she ranted while the old man calmly carried on eating.

Then she said: 'Yuk! Toffee's been walking over that floor.'

My ears pricked up. Yuk? What do you mean, 'yuk'? I'll have you know I spent ten minutes this morning cleaning my paws. You could eat off my paws. My paws are cleaner than a sterilised piccalilli pickle jar.

The old man smiled. Wiped his hands down the side of his trousers and said: 'Don't worry. I kept to the five second rule.'

'Which is....?' she asked.

'If you drop something on the floor and pick it up within five seconds it's safe to eat. No bacteria. None. Zilch.'

'That is patently ridiculous,' the old woman replied. 'If you get botulism and die a horrible death, rolling around in agony, it'll be your own fault.' With that she filled a bucket with water and what looked like a gallon of disinfectant and got the mop.

'Horse. Bolted.' said the old man, a comment which only made the old woman go redder and start scrubbing the floor as if she were expecting a visit from half a dozen crawling fragile babies.

If you have a dog – poor you if you do – there is a simple test to see whether dropped food is contaminated. Let the dog eat some of it, wait five seconds and then check if he's still alive.

March 14

It is evening and I have been home alone all day. Feel faint. Can't move. Eyes won't focus. As I lie flopped in front of my empty bowl I hear the old woman say to the old man, 'Did you feed Toffee this morning?'

He looks at me and nudges me with his toe. I don't move and start to pant slightly.

'Oh, Lord! She's only had one huge bowl of meaty chunks, a saucer of milk, a handful of treats and a bowl of biscuits to last her all day,' he says, and laughs. Is laughing an appropriate response? I think not.

'Oooo, the poor thing. I think she's starving to death,' says the old woman, who's laughing too. She goes to the fridge and pours something into the bowl.

'Here, Toffee, here's a snack for you.'

I leap to my feet and make a lunge for the bowl. PRAWNS. PRAWNS. PRAWNS. PRAWNS.

The old man shakes his head. 'She seems to have made a remarkable recovery.'

Yes, I have, thank you very much.

March 15

The old man's nephew Jack called round tonight. He's an idiot. He and his equally idiotic friends have formed a rock band called We Sound Like Six Dogs Howling At The Moon - or something like that.

He had his iPhone in his hand and was proudly telling the old man and the old woman about his last 'gig'. I don't know what a 'gig' is but it sounds like it could be an event where young people sing badly and annoy all the drinkers in a pub who have dropped in for a quick pint and a chat with their mates.

He was very excited because We Sound Like Six Dogs Howling At The Moon have another 'gig' lined up, this time at the football club.

I fear they will get a good kicking.

March 16

The old woman accused me of being selfish after I stretched out on the chair and refused to let her sit down.

Later I tried to prove I was kind and generous by dropping a dead bird I found in the garden into her bath. She leapt out of the tub and ran around the house shrieking, naked as the day she was born. Not a pretty sight.

The old man grabbed a towel to wrap her in - probably couldn't bear the sight of her either – and then removed the bird from the bath and pulled the plug.

The old woman is now having a shower.

My gift has been wrapped in newspaper and consigned to the rubbish bin.

I don't know why I bother.

March 17

It's St Patrick's Day today. He's the patron saint of Ireland. The old man and the old woman have been to Ireland twice; once for a long weekend in Dublin and the second time for a 10-day break in some ass end of beyond county where the only entertainment was one fiddle player in a pub with a woman dancer in short green dress trying to pretend she was the female version of Riverdance's Michael Flatley.

Both times the old man's niece Violet came to stay to 'baby-sit' me. The old man and the old woman would have been surprised at the shenanigans that went on while they were away. Let's just say they involved a young man, now her husband, several bottles of alcohol and getting 'nekkid'. I hot-footed it to the sitting-room sofa and hid my eyes under my paws but I couldn't block out the sound of what appeared to be two bellowing hippopotamuses fighting for supremacy in the mud of Mozambique.

The old man and the old woman always celebrate St Patrick's Day because the old woman claims she has Irish blood coursing through her veins after researching her family tree and finding out her great-great-great grandmother's maiden name was McNamara. In reality, it's just an excuse for going out and downing several pints of Guinness with their mates in some themed pub decorated with Irish flags and shamrocks.

I went out into the garden and ate quite a bit of grass. So my contribution to St Pat's Day will be throwing up copious amounts of green and white foam in front of the door just before they leave.

They'll like that.

March 18

I spent all morning sharpening my claws and spent all afternoon ripping open food pouches.

Hungry.

March 19

I was napping in the sitting-room when I heard someone say, 'What a gorgeous little floof!'

I opened one eye and there looking down at me was a woman who, it transpired, was a work colleague of the old woman's.

I didn't have a clue what she was talking about. I glanced around the room. I saw no floof. Then I realised she was staring at ME. ME. I am NOT a floof. I am not cute or fluffy. In no way could I be described as a floof. Why would anyone call me a floof? Why? Why?

Her hand came towards me, presumably to stroke my floofiness. I unleashed my claws. The old woman saw the claws emerge and the look in my eye and swooped like an eagle who'd spotted a mouse and swept me up.

'She's not very good with strangers,' she said nervously. 'I'll put her in the kitchen.'

She walked out with me, holding my two front paws as I wriggled to escape. She got to the kitchen and put me down. Luckily for her I saw her reach into the fridge where she found some left over beef from last night's tea.

'Here you are Toffee. Now behave yourself, please.'

I'll behave myself as long as it takes me to eat this beef. But when I returned to the sitting-room, the door was firmly closed.

March 20

I had a slight argument with a laundry basket today. There it was full of clean soft clothes so, naturally, I had to lie on them. I pushed my paw through the slat in the side…and couldn't get it back again. I tugged and wriggled. The basket fell over on its side. I scrabbled in the clothes and tugged some more. The laundry basket ended up on the other side of the room, leaving a trail of clothes, before I finally extricated my paw. I retired to the bedroom to lick my wounds.

When the old woman came home she started shouting until her voice reached a pitch that only dogs can hear.

'Toffee! What have you done to the laundry? It was clean when I left this morning and now look at! I shall have to wash it all over again.'

That's right, worry about the clothes, why don't you? Don't worry about me with my poorly paw. I could have been seriously injured.

SERIOUSLY INJURED.

March 21

The old woman is on a healthy eating regime. Luckily it

hasn't affected me but the old man is getting mightily pissed off. It was the old woman's turn to do the packed lunches this morning. When the old man came home from work he said, 'Celery sticks! For God's sake. Celery sticks. I don't want bloody celery sticks in my packed lunch! I hate celery. I've always hated celery. I haven't miraculously overnight turned into a celery lover. NO MORE CELERY!'

I don't think he likes celery.

March 22

The old man and the old woman were looking at a picture of a weird looking kitten with a big head and a vacant look in its eyes. It has just been adopted by her friend.

I was briefly worried. Surely they wouldn't consider trading me in for a younger model, would they?

I put my paw on the old woman's leg and looked up at her with my most appealing expression.

'Has Toffee got indigestion?' asked the old man

'Are you feeling poorly, Toffee?' asked the old woman.

They both cuddled me and she said, 'We wouldn't want anything bad to happen to you, would we?' and the old man ruffled my ears.

Phew, I think I've dodged a bullet there.

March 23

I'm in trouble for pinching some fresh tuna off the kitchen table.

Sorry.

Not sorry.

March 24

The old man brought a nice cup of tea into the sitting-room and settled down to watch something 'exciting' on the tellybox. His idea of 'exciting' means programmes about building 'megastructures', watching men drive trucks on ice or people selling things they found in a lock-up storage facility. Yawn.

He was so engrossed in the tellybox he neglected his cup of tea. As you know, I always strive to be as helpful as possible so I put my paw in it to test the temperature.

I swished my paw about a bit, licked it off (I can report tea is vile) and put it back into make sure it was still vile. The old man spotted what I was doing. Was he grateful? He was not.

'For goodness sake, Toffee. That is DISGUSTING!' he yelled and stalked into the kitchen to throw it away.

What is his problem?

March 25

If I kindly sit on your feet to keep them warm, I WILL ATTACK IF YOU MOVE THEM.

March 26

There I was lying on the sofa, minding my own business, when I spotted the old man and the old woman advancing towards me, he carrying a towel and she with her hands behind her back.

Suddenly they were upon me, the old man wrapped me in the towel and the old woman produced...oh no, NAIL CLIPPERS! They seem to think that every once in a while my nails require a slight trimming. The old man grasped my paw and held it out to the old woman. She pounced and - clip! - one tip of a nail gone. I was so shocked I did nothing. I just lay in the old man's arms and let the old woman trim my nails one by one.

'Toffee's being very good,' said the old woman.

This comment brought me to my senses. Toffee/Good - these two words do NOT go together. My acquiescence must have lulled them into a false sense of security. Using the element of surprise, I yowled, wriggled free of the towel and scrabbled out of the old man's arms, catching him and the old woman with my one remaining claw.

I am now back on the sofa with 17 of my 18 claws vandalised beyond all recognition. I yawned and used my untouched 18th claw to scratch behind my ears, giving a secret smile as I looked at the old man and the old woman sitting stony-faced with plasters on their hands.

Serve them right.

March 27

EEK! Do you *mind* not walking into a room carrying a rustling paper bag? You know I am of a nervous disposition.

March 28

I was feeling restless today. I went out and sat in the garden for two minutes but it was cold so I came back in again. I sat on the sofa for a few seconds and then decided I needed fresh air and hoped the weather had turned a little warmer.

Once outside, I thought it was too cold after all and came back in again. I then paced around for a bit, trying to decide what to do next. I hovered in front of the cat flap and then eyed up the sofa. Or should I go and lie on the bed? Or sleep under the rosebush?

The old man was reading his newspaper and watching my comings and goings. He peered over the top.

'You know what Louis Camuti said, don't you, Toffee?'

Who's Louis Camuti when he's at home?

The old man wasn't going to shut up in a hurry.

'He said, most cats when they are out want to be in, and vice versa, and often simultaneously.' He then laughed as if he'd cracked some hilarious joke.

The man is a dingbat.

March 29

The old man and the old woman invited some new friends around for dinner tonight. I kept out of the way for a while but I could hear laughter and the sound of glasses clinking at the dining table.

Then the smell of roast chicken wafted past my nostrils and I decided to make an entrance just in case there was any going spare. I sashayed up to the dining table and sat expectantly staring up at the women guest.

'Oh,' she said. 'Oh dear, a cat! I'm not good with cats, would you mind ...?'

The old man leapt to his feet.

'I'm sorry, I'll take her out.'

He carried me into the sitting-room

'Sorry, old girl,' he said as he closed the door.

To say I was annoyed was an understatement. I paced about, scratched at the door a few times and meowed annoyingly for a while - all to no avail. Eventually, the door opened and the old woman came in with a big bowl of chicken.

'Here you are, Toffee,' she said, as she rubbed my ears.

The old man popped his head around the door.

'They're not coming again,' he said as he bent down to ruffle my fur.

'No, definitely not,' said the old woman.

I snaffled up the chicken and purred.

Everything is back to normal.

March 30

I don't mind the occasional ballad but most hooman music leaves me cold. When the old woman is out, The old man occasionally plays songs by people called Deep Purple, Black Sabbath and Whitesnake. Today he was playing air guitar while stomping around the sitting-room banging his head up and down. The volume was deafening and I skedaddled out into the garden - although I'd need to skedaddle several miles away if I wasn't to hear it at all.

The old woman' tastes are little more 'quiet'. She plays people like Mumford And Sons (strange emotional wailing), Bruce Springsteen (strange loud wailing) and Taylor Swift (strange female wailing).

My favourite song is Food Glorious Food.

March 31

It was cold today so I snuggled up in the duvet and slept, arising only once to have a mouthful of food and a quick trip to the garden to answer a call of nature. The rest of time of I was chasing rabbits and shredding cardboard boxes in my dreams.

The old man and the old woman came home in the evening after spending a busy day at work. They had been caught up in traffic and were late. Poor things, they looked exhausted. I slept curled up on the old man's lap while they watched the tellybox. Both kept yawning, so loudly that it temporarily roused me from my nap. Then it was an early night for both of them.

So naturally at around midnight, I awoke, full of the joys of spring. I sprinted around the house to find things to play with. Luckily there was a coathanger on the bedroom floor, which was soon removed from between my paws by a bleary-eyed old man.

The old woman's feet were sticking out from under the duvet so I pounced. She screamed and withdrew these playthings back under the duvet. I slept for an hour before waking again. The dressing table seemed a little untidy to my eyes, so I tried to rearrange it. Unfortunately, several things fell with a clatter to the floor.

The old man and the old woman both sat bolt upright and put the light on. By then I was back on the bed curled up in a ball.

There followed a big kerfuffle about burglars and whether they were or were not downstairs legging it with various electronic products and the contents of the old woman's handbag – a packet of extra strong mints, sundry items of used make-up, two biros and £4.23 in loose change. The old man was despatched to investigate armed with the coathanger I had been playing with earlier. What was he going to do with that? Offer to hang up the burglars' jackets while they removed the handbag, one old laptop, the tellybox and a Sky box?

Having ascertained all their ancient equipment was still intact, they went back to sleep, only for the alarm to wake them an hour later.

They awoke with bloodshot eyes and hair standing on end.

I am living with zombies.

APRIL

April 1

The old woman was poring over the internet again and looking at sites featuring 'famous' cats like Cole and Marmalade and Lil Bub. I meowed crossly. It's not that I'm jealous of their fame and fortune, you understand, but that I too could so EASILY do what they do - easy peasy while standing on my head.

I know I'm not exactly *looking* for a job. It would be a bit difficult to fit it in what with me sleeping 18 hours a day, and the rest of the time eating, pooping and licking my bum. Even so, it's the PRINCIPLE that counts.

April 2

The trouble with the old man is that he thinks he's funny but his humour doesn't always go down well with the old woman. This evening she had on a new dress and was twirling about in front of the mirror.

'I'm not sure about this. What do you think, Toffee?' I shut my eyes and pretended to be asleep. It was dark red and a bit tight. She looked like a salami whose skin was about to burst.

The old man looked out from behind the newspaper he was reading.

'You look really hot, babe,' he said.

The old woman smiled. 'Thank you!'

'Yeah, you must be really sweating in that cheap polyester.'

That was two hours ago and she hasn't spoken to him since.

He keeps repeating, 'I was JOKING. It was a JOKE!' It's going to take more than that, old man.

April 3

The old man claims I'm getting a little chubby. Pot. Kettle. Black. Are three words that spring to mind.

I didn't take the slightest bit of notice until I walked into the sitting-room and he shouted, 'Watch out! Wide load approaching!'

That does it. I'm going to eat less and exercise more.

April 4

I spent all night exercising. Down the stairs, up the stairs, twice around the bedroom. Repeat. Repeat. Repeat.

The old man and the old woman got up with bleary eyes and kept yawning.

'That cat is a menace,' said the old man. Menace? It was you who said I was getting chubby.

Jeez, they're hard to please.

April 5

I've just heard the old man asking the old woman if she'd seen the cheese and biscuits he'd left on the table.

'I saw them earlier,' she said. Then they both looked at me licking my lips while sitting on three crackers.

'WHAT? You think it was me? Why blame me? I always get the blame. Give me a break.' I could have said more but I was too busy digging pieces of cheddar out of my teeth.

April 6

I try to educate myself and learn a new word every day. I learnt one today when the old man stubbed his toe as he was coming out of the bathroom. But I don't think I am ever going to use in polite company.

April 7

Mrs Hartley gave the old man and the old woman a cooked crab. Her son had given her a two and she was sharing the love.

The old woman said she was going to make crab cakes 'just like those ones we had in that little bistro in France'. The old man looked a bit dubious, opened his mouth to say something but spotted the look in her eyes and shut up. Very wise. And off he went to work.

The old woman rolled up her sleeves and put on her novelty apron, the one that says A Meal Without Wine Is Called Breakfast - appropriate for her, except I don't think they should have excluded breakfast.

She looked at the crab and it looked right back at her. She must have realised she didn't have a clue what to do so she found a Youtube video with all the instructions. What a palaver. It involved pulling off the claws and legs and cracking them open with a hammer. She's a bit heavy-handed so spent the next half an hour picking splintered shell out of the meat.

Removing the body from the shell involved a huge knife and twisting to separate the two parts of the body. I hid for that process; I had visions of being skewered on the kitchen door. Then she had to pick off something called 'dead man's fingers'.

It was all very fiddly and time-consuming. At the end of two hours there was a small pile of white crab meat and some sloppy brown crab meat. Crab juice was sloshing about all over the place and there were shell shards and splinters covering the table. It looked like the crab had exploded.

Then it was back to the laptop to find a recipe for crab cakes.

Soooo, the old woman was out of the room. There was crab in a bowl. There was one hungry cat. And there I was having a lick of the crab – yum, delish - when the old woman walked back in the room.

'TOFFEE!' she yelled, scooping me up and dumping me on the floor. She stared at the crab and opened the bin. Then shut it again muttering something about, 'What the eye doesn't see...'

Four hours later the old man came home from work. He looked in the fridge and there were four crab cakes on a plate. He looked impressed.

'They don't take long to cook,' said the old woman, as she bustled about finishing off the dinner.

She dished up potato, vegetables and crab cakes on to the old man's plate. Hers was the same, minus the crab cakes.

'Aren't you having any?' he asked.

'You know what it's like, you spend all day cooking something and you kind of lose your appetite.'

'You don't know what you're missing!'

'I think I do,' she said, glancing in my direction.

'What?'

'Nothing, darling. I'm just glad you're enjoying them.'

Shameless.

April 8

The old man sat down to watch the tellybox. I jumped on him immediately and cuddled up under his chin. I thought his new black jumper would be much improved by the addition of lots of ginger hair. From the way he was frantically brushing himself down later, I don't think he agreed.

Can't win 'em all, old man.

April 9

The old woman was dashing about this morning like a blue-arsed fly on speed. She'd overslept, tripped over a cat toy *someone* had left at the bottom of the stairs... and lost a folder of papers which she only found when *someone* got up from the sofa to stretch her legs and investigate her food bowl.

'Toffee!' she huffed,' You're a pest.'

I yawned.

'It's OK for you, you don't have to go to work, do shopping, do housework - and LOOK AFTER A GREAT LUMP OF A GINGER CAT!'

I wanted to tell her all about my busy days of sleeping, eating, pooping, hunting and playing but she'd gone, sprinting (if you can call her lumbering gait sprinting) through the door dragging the poor old man with her.

April 10

The old man and the old woman were watching a tellybox programme about dogs sniffing out drugs in airports. There they were, sniffing their arses and then the suitcases - the dogs, that is, not the old man and the old woman. This soppy pair sat on the sofa oohing and aahing.

'Oo, aren't they intelligent?'

'Ahh, I'm sure he's smiling.'

'Oo, what a clever dog!'

'Ahh, he's gone straight for that woman's crotch.'

Yeah, well. The reason why I am never going to schlepp around some airport, showing off, is because I AM NOT A GRASS. I am not a little tattle-tale. I am not a stool pigeon.

I leave all that kind of thing to those toadying, desperate-to-please yappers.

THAT. IS. ALL.

April 11

Today has been full of peculiar happenings.

The old man was singing in the bath so I hopped onto the side to listen. I sat at the end of the bath sitting bolt upright and stared unblinkingly at him. He immediately stopped singing - not only that he immediately put his hands over his lower front.

Why? Why?

I later heard him telling the old woman: 'There is something seriously wrong with that cat.' Not a clue which cat he was talking about.

I wandered downstairs and ate my salmon in jelly, plus some dead flies tangled up in cobwebs. I think the salmon upset my delicate stomach because I threw up all over a chair.

The next thing I knew all the food in my bowl had DISAPPEARED. Where is it? Has it dematerialised? Why is the old man gently rubbing my tummy?

Feeling a bit stressed, I went into the sitting-room and started knocking books off the coffee table. The next thing I knew I was whisked out of the room and the door magically remained shut to me all day.

This afternoon I went for nap. No sooner had I fallen asleep and my bed was snatched from under me. What was going on? That basket of clean clothes was so comfy.

So all in all it's been a weird kind of a day.

April 12

I had an important decision to make today. Should I present the dead mouse I had hidden in the garden to the old man and the old woman at 2am or 5am? I decided on 5am. I expect they were grateful for the gift and the opportunity to get an early start to the day.

Timing is all.

April 13

The old woman made Sticky Toffee Pudding today. It was too sweet for me - I know because I had a crafty lick when no one was looking. I also know it was 'sticky' because most of it is now stuck to a velvet cushion and my fur.

Oops!

April 14

The old man is furious with me for dropping his headphones down the toilet. I'm only trying to train him to keep the lid down.

The saphead.

April 15

The old man and the old woman were sitting at the computer in deep discussion. Occasionally they'd look up and stare at me. I didn't like it one bit so I strolled over to see what was occupying their attention.

Turned out they were doing one of those quizzes. This one was called Is Your Cat Brainy or Brain Dead?

I was offended. Surely they already knew they were living with a ginger genius. If there is a meltdown in society forget about survivalism and stockpiling tins of beans and bear-traps. Instead, tie yourself to a cat - for what animal is better equipped to survive whatever the odds?

It's very nice of the old man and the old woman to feed me, shelter me and care for me but, if the chips are down, I know I can skip out the front door, find food to eat and, more importantly, soon hook up with the one person in the neighbourhood with an underground shelter, a generator, his own well and a couple of thousand cans of meaty chunks. See, genius.

Just look at my computer skills. I can walk across a keyboard and the next day a packet of balloons shaped like animals, four iPads and The Complete Works of William Shakespeare will arrive from Amazon. See, genius.

Then there are my shape-shifting abilities. I weigh about 11lbs (5kg) and yet I can oust those two hulks I live with to a tiny corner of the bed where they hang on for dear life. That's because overnight I turn into a 150lb (68kg) panther. See, genius.

Modesty precludes me from mentioning all my other genius abilities. Anyway, the results of this test were: 'You are living with a feline Einstein! Your cat is extremely intelligent and continually amazes you with new tricks. Your cat also knows how to get you to do things their way. You're going to need to be pretty crafty yourself if you want to outsmart your cat!'

Yes, I am a genipuss.

April 16

Today I made a list of all the things that should be banned. It includes: dogs, closed doors, dogs, pills, dogs, quorn (and any food that LOOKS like meat but isn't), dogs, whistles, dogs, visitors, dogs, smiling, smiling dogs, inappropriate petting, dogs, and Rajah/Percy. Oh, and dogs. .

April 17

If you want me to use one of the ten scratching posts scattered around the house, then put them nearer to me.

Use your head, peeps.

April 18

The old man has a couple of days off work and for once the old woman hasn't left him a list of chores as long as my tail. He pottered around for a bit and tidied up. He made the bed and did some dusting.

Then he went outside and came in from the shed carrying several cardboard boxes and for the next couple of hours made me an elaborate castle complete with cut-out turrets and a drawbridge.

I love that man.

April 19

The castle is still largely intact although there are a few places where 'someone' has nibbled out a few holes.

This evening the old woman caught the old man licking mint sauce off his lamb chops and feeding me chunks of meat. She said, 'You spoil that cat.'

Spoil? Such treatment is my due.

April 20

Today the old woman decided she was going to clear out the attic. I know what her clearing binges are like so kept well clear. I didn't want to end up in a black bin bag and carted off to the dump.

She was banging away up there and then came the sound of something being dragged, like a dead body being moved in a horror film. I blocked up my ears with my paws but couldn't ignore the noise as items came thumping through the loft door.

I gingerly went to investigate, keeping one eye on the opening. I didn't want to get brained by a box of sundry items. There were old clothes, kitchen equipment that would never toast, grill, chop or steam again, books and broken ornaments (if they were weren't broken before they were by the time they smashed into the landing).

She peered through the opening.

'Well, Toffee, I haven't found an old masterpiece yet, but I live in hopes. Keep back, girl, here comes a big one.'

I shifted pretty damn quick as a box came sliding down the loft ladder and clattered to the floor with a horrendous hullabaloo. I peeked inside and saw tools. The old man's tools. I smell trouble.

The old man came home and was at first impressed by the old woman's exertions but then he spotted the box of tools. All hell broke loose.

'What are doing with my tools!' he yelled. 'You're not throwing those out.'

'Yes I am, you never use them,' she yelled back.

'Of course I use them. How do you think the boiler got mended?'

'What, after you knocked it about a bit with a hammer and made it a hundred times worse? It was mended by THE PLUMBER.'

'I need those tools, woman.'

Then started a tussle between the two of them as each tried to claim the box.

I decided to leave them to it.

By bedtime an uneasy truce had prevailed. One or two of the obviously more broken tools were out with the rubbish, while the rest were stowed away in a new box ready to go back into the attic.

That's the problem, to the old woman it's rubbish, to the old man it's spare parts.

April 21

The old woman looked up from her laptop and said, 'I'm an ailurophile.' The old man snorted, gulped and spluttered. A man of few words but many noises.

'It means I love cats,' she added.

He gasped, said 'phew' and laughed.

April 22

I have invented a new game. I call it WhackaRat. It's quite simple. While the old woman was sitting on the sofa reading I whacked my toy mouse on to the cupboard door where it made a satisfying thump. Thump. Thump. Thump. Thump. Thump. Thump. Thump. Thump. Thump. Thump. Thump. Thump. Thump. Thump. Thump. Thump. Thump. Thump. Thump.

'FOR GOODNESS SAKE, TOFFEE, WILL STOP THAT INFERNAL RACKET. I'M TRYING TO READ.'

Jeez. There's no need to shout.

April 23

I may occasionally sound slightly grumpy but I do appreciate my staff. The Help do their very best for me despite their limitations. I expect good service and on the whole I get it.

In return, they are well paid with guard duties (I always let them know vociferously when there is an interloper in the garden) and entertainment. They are always laughing at me. 'Here comes Toffee's funny five minutes,' they say, demonstrating how much they appreciate my comedy routine.

However, yesterday they let me down but, even worse, they let themselves down.

As you may have noticed, spring is springing so the old man and old woman have had a couple of days' holiday in order to get out into the garden. They have started tilling so many vegetable seeds and seedlings that you might suspect there is a famine just around the corner and they want to be prepared. I haven't seen the cat mint going in yet but no doubt it's just an oversight which will be remedied shortly.

I curled up on a bag of compost in the shed, peering out of the door to keep an eye on them. They always need me to supervise. It's what I do best. It was a sunny day and as I was relaxing I thought I would 'rest my eyes' for a while. The next thing I knew, that shed door banged shut and I was TRAPPED.

I must have been there for HOURS AND HOURS, although I later heard the old woman telling the old man, 'I don't know why she's making so much fuss, she was only in there 20 minutes.' I think it was a slip of the tongue and she meant hours...or possibly days.

Anyway, I yowled and scratched and then jumped up on the bench and pressed my face to the window to see if I could attract anyone's attention.

When they FINALLY let me out, I stalked off in a right old strop. This made them laugh. They're so stupid they can't even tell the difference between a justifiable sulk and one of my comedy routines.

I took myself off to the spare bedroom where I stayed for the rest of the day, punishing them by not allowing them my company. I saw later that they had tried to drown their sorrows by drinking lots of red wine and beer and watching the tellybox.

They are obviously contrite so I have forgiven them but they should know they are ON A WARNING and should anything similar happen again I might not be so forgiving.

April 24

Today I helped with the laundry. The old woman had washed, dried and folded it. There it sat in the laundry basket, waiting to be ironed. I thought I'd be helpful and try to remove the creases by sitting on it. I slept on that white shirt all day. When she got home, the old woman sighed. 'Look at the state of this shirt, Toffee. Your grubby hairs are all over it. I'll have to wash it again.' Grubby? Me? How very dare she.

I stalked out of the room. That's the last time I try to help with the housework - unless you can see any prawns that need hoovering up.

April 25

Me (sitting by full food bowl): Meow, meow, meow.

The old woman: Your bowl is full.

Me: Meow, meow, meow.

The old woman: I thought you were hungry.

Me: Meow, meow, meow.

I give her The Stare.

Me: Meow, meow, meow.

The old woman: Oh, all right then, here's some prawns.

I sniff prawns, stick nose in air and walk away. I've changed my mind.

The old woman (shouting after me): 'You are the most spoilt cat that has ever walked this earth!'

And your point is ...?

April 26

The old woman brought home another toy. It's a wind-up mouse that buzzes about all over the place like a very annoying furry wasp.

I dutifully played with it for a few minutes while she watched. I don't want to discourage her from buying me presents. Later I carried the thing into the garden and buried it.

In the evening she asked, 'Where's Toffee's mouse? She really loved it and now I can't see it anywhere.'

The old man picked up cushions, looked under the sofa and ran his hand across the top of the bookcase. 'God knows what's happened to that,' he said.

The old woman sighed. 'Toffee's things just disappear in this house. I think she must have a wand, just like Harry Potter.'

'Don't you mean Hairy Potter?' said the old man and they both fell about laughing.

Not even vaguely amusing.

April 27

The old woman caught me licking her toothbrush. It wasn't unpleasant; kinda minty. I thought she'd be pleased that I was cleaning it. But, no. It's now soaking in a glass of neat disinfectant.

I don't know why.

April 28

I killed an alien invader today. Did I get any thanks? No, I did not. Just the old man yelling: 'Toffee, what the bloody hell have you done to my shoe?'

April 30

Rajah/Percy's been here again, creeping over the fence, winding around the garden shed. He walked around with his nose and tail in the air. The blockhead.

I watched him from behind a shrub. He settled down under the bush near the bird table. I came flying across the garden, growling all the way. His fur stood on end and he growled back but soon legged it back over the fence.

I am victorious. Yet again. Toffee rules.

MAY

May 1

The old woman has been given a book of poems and sayings about cats. She started reading one out to the old man by somebody called Swinburne.

Stately, kindly, lordly friend,
Condescend
Here to sit by me, and turn
Glorious eyes that smile and burn,
Golden eyes, love's lustrous mead,
On the golden page I read.

I carried on licking my bum. They both looked at me and burst out laughing.

I wonder about them sometimes.

May 2

The old woman is still trawling through that damn book and read out this Mark Twain quote: 'If man could be crossed with the cat it would improve the man, but it would deteriorate the cat.'

I was at that moment trying to fit into a small cardboard box and breaking out the sides.

'I don't think Twain ever had a cat,' said the old man.

What's that supposed to mean? Is that an insult? I think it's an insult.

May 3

The old woman picked up Mr Fluffy Bum by one leg and tossed him into the bin. I immediately ran to the bin and knocked it over, rescuing my best friend and carrying him into the sitting-room. I gave him a cuddle on the sofa and hissed as the old woman tried to retrieve him.

She looked at me. 'It's OK, Toffee. I won't bin him, I didn't realise you loved him so much.'

May 4

When I got up this morning, Mr Fluffy Bum looked like a new toy. He had been stitched, washed and brushed.

Aw thanks, old woman.

May 5

What can I say? I like to climb trees. High up in the branches I have a good vantage point of the surrounding area. I can see the undergrowth shaking if there is a little creature scuttling in it. I can pounce if I feel like it although usually I can't be bothered. I can sharpen my claws on the trunk. I can look starlings in the eye and laugh at their frightened screeches as they fly away, grumbling about why a cat is on their perch.

I am a brilliant climber.

Unfortunately, I am not always a brilliant getting-downer.

So it was that yesterday I was surveying my kingdom from the top of the oak tree at the bottom of the garden. I had soothed an itch by rubbing my back on the rough bark. I had honed my claws to perfection. I had frightened four starlings, three sparrows, a blackbird and a cluster of bluetits. All in all a good hour's work.

I began to get sleepy and knew I mustn't drop off on the branch or I would, well - drop off. I stepped onto the branch below - so far so good - and then onto the one below that. That's when the trouble started. I heard a long crack followed by a short sharp one and the whole branch sheared away. I managed to get to another branch in the nick of time. Oh Lord. I don't mind admitting I was a tad concerned. The next available stepping place seemed an awfully long way away.

I meowed. Nothing.

What were the old man and the old woman doing? Why

weren't they concerned about the whereabouts of their most treasured possession? ME!

Long story short. They EVENTUALLY realised I was missing. The old man got a ladder out of the shed and just as he reached the top of it I had the brilliant idea of stepping sideways and then down and I nimbly shimmied swiftly to the ground.

Honestly. What language - tut, tut, tut.

'I don't know why I bloody bother!' he yelled.

The old woman made a big fuss of me and I could see she was trying not to laugh at the old man. He put the ladder away and stalked indoors. I took myself off to the spare bedroom to sleep off the trials of my day. And to keep out of the way of the old man's stomping feet.

May 6

I was on the sofa sitting on an open magazine.

'I swear Toffee can read,' said the old woman.

'What? Through her arse?' said the old man.

The man's a fool.

May 7

SEND HELP. I HAVE BEEN KIDNAPPED.

This is not a joke. I was sleeping peacefully on the sofa when someone grabbed me and put me into a carrier thingy. They were clever - very, very clever. I could see out of the carrier a little bit and whoever had taken me was wearing trousers just like the old man's. His accomplice had disguised her voice to sound like the old woman.

The kidnappers were obviously trying to lull me into a false sense of security but they didn't fool me, the old man and the old woman would never subject me to this treatment.

The next thing I knew I was in a car and being driven away. I could hear bits of a conversation over the sound of the car engine. I heard: 'She's not gonna to like it,' and 'Do you think she will ever forgive us?' and 'It's for her own good.' Being kidnapped is for my own good? I don't think so.

Then I was in a place that smelled strongly medicinal. I could

hear people talking about dreadful subjects like cat flu and cali-
civirus and, worst of all - gulp - INJECTIONS. I was taken from
the carrier and plonked unceremoniously on a metal table.
Someone had me covered with a towel - someone wearing very
thick gloves.

Now, here I am and - I hardly know how to tell you this - a man
in a white coat is STICKING NEEDLES INTO MY REAR END. What
torture is this?

As my head emerges from under the towel I see the old man
and the old woman. They have come to rescue me! The old
woman picks me up and strokes me. The old man tickles me
under the chin. Stop faffing about, you two.

RUN, RUN!

May 8

After yesterday's indignities, the old man and the old woman
have been spoiling me. I am grateful to them for rescuing me
from Mad Needle Man but that doesn't stop me from trying to
make capital from the situation.

I'm actually feeling pretty well but I have finally perfected
the 'I'm feeling really poorly' look and I thought today was a
good time to try it out.

I dragged myself up onto the sofa and then lay there with my
eyes open.

The old man picked me up and I flopped in his arms.

'Do you think she's all right?' he asked.

The old woman looked worried.

'I hope she's not allergic to the jabs,' she said. 'I'll see if she'll
eat.'

She brought in a handful of fresh prawns. I ate them in 10 seconds flat and meowed for more. She eyed me suspiciously.

'Mmm, she seems to be bearing up remarkably well,' she said.

Has anyone ever told her sarcasm is the lowest form of wit?

May 9

I was playing a new game which involved running at full pelt
into the sitting-room, stopping abruptly and sliding across the

floor.

The old woman said, 'Do you think we should take her to a cat behaviour counsellor?'

What's that when it's at home? No time to think about it now. 'WHEEEE!'

May 10

Hooman hair is an acquired taste. I had a chew on the old man's in the middle of the night. He twitched a bit in his sleep but didn't wake.

This morning he surveyed a few strands on the pillow and said to the old woman, 'Oh my God. I think I've started to go bald!'

If it had tasted better, you soon would be.

May 11

Birds. What are they about? What is the point of them? They flap about making weird chirping noises, sit in trees and make a mess on the ground. Useless.

Why did the old man and the old woman set up a bird table in the garden? It only encourages the little twerps. I know it's good fun leaping at them and chasing them. Their chirps turn to squawks then - but I could live without this little amusement.

Yesterday I was even more pissed off with them than usual. I was lying on the windowsill catching a few rays when this blackbird landed on a tree outside and started chirruping away. Annoyed at having my sleep interrupted, I leapt up to catch it… and hit my head on the window. Yes, folks, the window was shut.

I fell behind the sofa. And all I could hear was that darn bird singing some stupid bloody song and, what was worse, he had been joined by a few other members of his flipping feathered family. Look, I was dazed. I was tired. I was angry… I had forgotten about the closed window.

So I got up and again tried to jump through that closed window.

This was all bad enough but then I heard laughter. The old

man was watching me from the doorway.

I stalked out of the room with my tail held high, as if it was something I had intended all along.

May 12

The old man and the old woman returned from the supermarket. I'm not sure all went well. The old woman is taking things out of bags and slamming them down on the table.

'It was just a JOKE,' the old man is wailing. 'Can't you take a JOKE!'

It seems when the check-out girl asked them if they wanted to buy A Bag For Life, the old man told her, 'I married mine.'

When will he ever learn?

May 13

'I tell you that cat is psychic,' said the old woman.

The old man looked at her dubiously. 'Really?'

'For a start she knows when I'm coming home. She's always sitting by her food bowl, whatever time of day.'

'Ye-esss. You don't think it's because she hears you coming?'

'No, darling, it's because she *senses* me coming.'

Of course, that and the fact she makes enough noise to wake the dead as she lumbers up the garden path and fumbles about putting the key in the lock.

May 14

Today I have practised the art of contemplative yoga (i.e. sleeping), followed by advanced relaxation techniques (i.e. sleeping) with a stretch of delta wave recognition (i.e. sleeping) and somnolent data recognition (i.e. sleeping and dreaming). Now I am on high alert as I've heard the front door open. The old man and the old woman are back from work so I must jump to it and comfort them as they relax on the sofa - by curling up between them and sleeping.

May 15

The old man and the old woman were trying to work out how many hours I sleep in a day. Do they not realise that when they are out I am a hive of activity? I have chores to do, like watching birds, eating meaty chunks, female grooming and keeping monsters away from the house.

Tonight when the old man came home from work I was asleep. I swear I had only nodded off a few seconds after an extremely busy day had exhausted me.

I leapt to my feet and stared under the sofa, tail swishing, as if I'm stalking creepy-crawlies.

'You don't fool me, Toffee,' says the old man, rubbing my ears. 'There's a cat-shaped depression in the cushion.'

Damn.

May 16

The old man said I had the attention span of a retarded gnat. How dare he. I'm so angry I could...

Oo, what's that just flown past the window? Going to jump on the windowsill. Who's left that rubber band on the sofa? Must twang it. Is that Mr Fluffy Bum in the corner? Come here and play.

What was the old man saying? Something about my short attention span. I do not have a short attention span, I'm just good at multi-tasking.

May 17

This evening I sat with the old man and the old woman as they watched a documentary about the Middle Ages.

There was a segment about medieval instruments of torture - all pretty gruesome stuff with racks, screws, pokers and spikes all featuring prominently. I shut my eyes. I am a cat of delicate sensibilities and didn't want to see those things.

I wished I could have shut my ears to the screaming - not screams from people being tortured but the screams of the old woman.

She's got a nerve, pretending to be so squeamish. Only last week she was torturing me with the cat brush trying to get burrs out of my coat that I had picked up from a patch of goose grass.

Torture? Those medieval men were all amateurs compared

to her.

May 18

Don't throw out this cardboard box I am sleeping in. I am aware it's far too small for me and I've broken out the sides.

I SAID DON'T THROW IT AWAY.

May 19

Is there no end to the cruelties I have to endure? This morning the old man and the old woman disappeared for the day leaving Mr Fluffy Bum on the top shelf of the bookcase. They put him there yesterday evening to stop me tearing around the house playing with him while they were trying to watch the tellybox.

I've tried getting him down. Serves them right that I've knocked books and knick-knacks onto the floor.

Ooops! I've always hated that porcelain hedgehog thing. I think I've done them a favour.

May 20

The old woman is obsessed by cookery programmes. She watches them all with a notebook by her side.

The old man hardly reacts to her incessant questions. Do you like boiled ostrich? Do you think rocket goes with strawberry jam? Do you think Randy's on his way out after what he did to that celebrity chef with that rolling pin? He knows no matter how many hours of programmes she's watched or pages of notes she's made, it'll still be nothing more elaborate than pork chops, peas and mashed potato for dinner.

But the other day, wonder of wonders, there she was in the kitchen with her notebook open in front of her and piles of ingredients beside her. I had my eye on a huge chicken lying on the chopping board. The old woman peered at it suspiciously.

'I'm supposed to bone this, Toffee,' she said, and waved her knife over it as if trying to magic the bones out.

'How do I do it?' I retreated under the table. I didn't fancy any of my bones being removed by accident. I didn't want to end up looking like a cat-shaped pyjama case.

I listened as she chopped, tore and swore at the poor old

chicken. Every so often I darted forward to snaffle up lumps that had dropped to the floor. Half an hour later I heard the sound of chicken being slapped into a baking tin so I crept out of my hiding place.

How did a chicken so big get transformed into so few small portions? What barbarism had taken place? I looked on the counter. There were bones and offal everywhere. It looked like an explosion in a butcher's shop. She piled a load into a saucepan to make something she called 'stock' but smelled more like 'sock' and swept the rest into the rubbish bin. She then started an attack on various vegetables. Carrots, fennel and onion were reduced to matchsticks by that mighty chopper. Herbs became dust and were incorporated into butter. The stock had been simmered and sieved and reduced to a puddle.

Then spices and flavourings were brought into play – a sprinkle here, a shake there.

The sweat was dripping from her brow and the kitchen looked as if it had been hit by a hurricane followed by a twister. There were pots and pans and stray pieces of food everywhere.

Eventually she removed the dish from the oven.

She took a taste and grimaced.

'Oh Lord,' she said, clutching at her throat. The chicken cooled and she tried to feed it to me. I made gagging noises so she pushed me out the back door. I stayed in the garden for ages, afraid to venture back into the battle zone.

Two hours later the old man came home from work. I tentatively poked my head through the cat flap. The kitchen was again clean and tidy. There were not unpleasant smells coming from the oven.

'What's for dinner?' the old man asked.

'Pork chop, peas and mashed potato.'

'Lovely!' he replied.

May 21

If you didn't want your ballpoint pen* to 'disappear', you shouldn't have left it on the coffee table.

Don't look under the sofa.
I SAID DON'T LOOK UNDER THE SOFA.
*Chew toy.

May 22

I had a bit of time on my paws today so I decided to become a poet. Here's my first attempt:

Ode To A Salmon
'Twas nice of you to swim about
In seas and up the river
But now you're sitting in a dish
About to be my dinner.

Brilliant, huh? I expect my work will soon be studied in schools and appearing on those Most Popular Poetry lists. I'm going to write another poem soon but I am an ARTISTE so I have to wait until the Muse visits me. I have a few things running around in my head. Does anyone know a word that rhymes with intestines?

Anyway, writing about salmon has made me hungry. Off now to investigate my food bowl. Then I shall take myself off to a soft duvet where I can contemplate the universe.

UniVERSE - get it?

God, I'm good.

May 23

My hooman pets were not appreciative of me singing to them in the middle of the night. I don't know why. I am the Beyoncé of cats.

May 24

'Slow down, Toffee. Anyone would think you hadn't been fed in a week.' The old man seems concerned at the speed at which I am inhaling my rabbit in jelly.

I look up and give him a withering look. I am STARVING because I haven't been fed for hours. At 7am my bowl contained chicken in gravy and a mound of dry biscuits. Then the old man and the old woman set off for work.

So apart from that, two woodlice, a spider, half a mouse, a half-eaten burger tossed into our garden by some half-wit on his way home from the takeaway and a lump of dried beef I found under the sofa, I HAVE EATEN NOTHING ALL DAY so excuse me for feeling a little peckish.

'She thinks she's a python and has to swallow everything whole,' the old man told the old woman.

She laughed but I was not amused.

There followed a lecture from the old man about the eating habits of a python. It seems they can consume quite large animals like antelope and monkeys. They squeeze the life out of the victim before eating it in one piece where it digests in the body.

Shudder…

The old man spotted me looking up at him.

'You, Toffee, would just be a tiny snack for a python, like me eating a peanut. But no doubt you'd be very tasty.'

Remind me never to visit a zoo.

May 25

Oh good, the old man has new shoes. The shoes are boring but the box is GREAT! If I can just wriggle myself into it…

May 26

Not a bad day today. The old man and the old woman were up before me and slid my chicken in jelly into my bowl as soon as I meowed at them. I'll train them yet.

It was then a quick trip out through the catflap for my morning constitutional before taking up position at the base of the bird table. Three dopey bluetits came a-calling. I launched myself up the bird table pole more in hope than expectation and they flapped away in dishevelled terror. Ha, ha, ha.

I strolled around spraying on the bushes to reiterate that this garden in MINE. But, do you know, that Rajah/Percy next door sidled sneakily over the fence.

I hurled myself at him and he hot-footed it pretty damn

quick.

I can't really remember much about the rest of the day. I had a nap on a pile of clean clothes folded neatly on the spare bed, turned round and round on it, messing it up nicely, before going outside to sit in the sun.

A couple of snacks and several naps later. The old man and the old woman were home from work. They do have their uses and scratching my stomach and rubbing my back are two of them.

Night, night peeps.

May 27

Thank you for my new scratching post, old man and old woman.

It's a sofa?

Same thing.

May 28

Today is the old man's birthday. I pressed my head against his and sang happy birthday to him at 3am. He was so happy he yelled and leapt out of bed.

May 29

The old woman is a bit of a wine lover and occasionally sips a glass or three as she is watching the soaps on the tellybox or working at her laptop. I have occasionally taken a sniff in the hope that by some miracle the wine has turned into gravy. Not happened yet.

The other evening she was sitting at her desk, a glass (huge tumbler) of vino at her side.

'Look at this, darling!' she yelled to the old man. 'This website has cat wine for sale.'

'You can't give wine to Toffee,' he said. 'She's mad enough without getting her drunk.'

Huh? Why drag me into this?

'It's not alcoholic; it's water infused with salmon and catnip.'

'So in no way does it resemble wine.'

'Well, it's called wine.'

'I could call tinned tuna, fillet steak, but it wouldn't be fillet steak, would it?'

'Now you're being picky.'

'How much is it anyway?'

'£6 a bottle.'

'£6 a bottle? You could buy six bottles of your gut rot for that,' he said and burst out laughing.

'You think you're so funny, don't you?' She thought for a minute or two. 'I could probably get two bottles for six quid if it was on special offer in Big Bargains.'

As they watched the tellybox later, she said to the old man, 'I could make some cat wine myself. How hard can it be to infuse something fishy and herby into water?'

For the love of God, woman, NOOOOOOO.

May 30

If I ruled the world… Oh, hang on a minute. I do.

May 31

The sun is shining so I was out in the garden again today. It was lovely to feel the sun on my fur and I was soon fast asleep. But it wasn't so nice at around 8.30am when I was awoken by parents dragging their squalling brats to school.

I was stretched out on the path where it was warmest, in full view of the street. Parents and kids stopped, pointed and called, 'Puss, puss, puss,' as if I were going to get up to greet a total stranger who hadn't even got some kind of catty foodstuff in its hand.

Then I hit on a clever wheeze. I stretched out and twisted my body. Then, eyes wide open, fixed my stare on the garden fence while holding my breath.

'Mummy, mummy, there's a dead cat in that garden!' shouted a little girl. Then I suddenly leapt in the air and she screamed blue murder.

I'm liking this; I could keep it up for hours.

JUNE

June 1

I learned something interesting last night. The old man doesn't like me jumping up and down on his bladder at 3pm.

Sorree…

June 2

Mrs Hartley saw me playing dead in the garden the other day. She came and asked the old woman if I was OK. She said she was just about to go over and check on me when I got up and went indoors.

She tickled me under the chin and handed over a big bag of cat treats as a 'get well' present.

That woman is going up in my estimation.

June 3

It rained all day and the garden turned into a quagmire. It didn't stop me from inspecting my territory, though, or from digging in the wet earth looking for worms. But I am nothing if not fastidious so I made sure my paws were nice and clean by the time the old man and the old woman came home.

Cleaning paws is easy. All you have to do is find a basket of freshly laundered clothes and walk all over it a few times.

I don't why but the old woman was in a really bad mood this evening, flinging clothes into the washing-machine and muttering under her breath.

She must have had a bad day at work.

June 4

The old man rolled in from the pub just before midnight. The old woman had already gone to bed but I, in a miscalculation I soon came to regret, was still downstairs on the sofa when he staggered in.

'Toffee! Hello, girl.'

I shut my eyes in the vain hope he would bugger off and leave me alone.

'Toffee!'

He plonked himself down beside me and absentmindedly stroked my fur.

'How heavy are you?'

What? Why does he want to know that?

He wittered on. 'I'm pretty damn strong, y'know. Pretty. Damn. Strong.'

The next thing I knew he had lifted me high into the air and began hoisting me up and down like a barbell.

'See I could easily be a weightlifter.'

I twisted and leapt, dragging my claws down the front of his body as I fell to the floor.

Strong? Do strong men cry?

This one did.

June 5

Who left that bag of frozen peas on the table? Who'd a thought they'd be so 'rolly'. The old man and the old woman are now chasing them all over the floor, stopping only to glare at me as I have a chew on the plastic bag they came in.

June 6

The old woman was plonked in front of her laptop again and, astonishingly, didn't need my help in finding interesting items on the internet.

All on her own she discovered a list of 'facts' about cats which she proceeded to read out to the old man and me. Despite the fascinating content, the old man didn't seem very excited and hid behind his newspaper from where he uttered the words, 'uh-uh' every so often, an all-purpose phrase which could mean either yes or no.

I don't know why he wasn't interested, some of these facts

were FASCINATING. For example, cats are the most popular pets in the world. I can't say I was surprised. There are three times more pet cats than pet dogs. THREE TIMES. Up yours, Fido.

Cats sleep an average of 15 hours a day. Amateurs. I can clock up 18 hours, no problem – more if the previous day has been particularly gruelling. Please note it's 'a day'. We may sleep for hours during daylight hours but then we are often up ALL NIGHT, protecting our hoomans from vampires and ghosts – and sharing the results of our hunting expeditions.

Then we got on to the tricky subject of weight. The average cat weighs about 4kg (8lb 13oz). This is true – up to a point. However, a cat's weight can fluctuate wildly. We are very heavy after scoffing a bowl of cat food, half the food on your plate, most of a mouse and 15 insects. Then we are very light after bringing it all up again, often in your shoes.

Cats are lethal and efficient hunters. True, but they are not so efficient at disposing of their prey, hence the need to put on footwear when you get up in the morning so you don't step on half a frog.

Cats love to play. This is especially true with kittens who love to chase toys and play fight. Play fighting among kittens is a way for them to practise and learn skills for hunting and fighting. Useful.

A group of cats is called a clowder, a male cat is called a tom, a female cat is called a molly or queen. This caused the old man to look up from his paper. 'Yeah, and Toffee is called a dictator with ideas above her station.'

NOW you decide to pay attention?

June 7

The eating habits of hoomans are very strange. They are addicted to this thing called 'sugar', which I can't even taste. They really love it and eat lots, even though they know it's not healthy.

Today I tried to help the old man and the old woman break this addiction. The old woman brought home a paper bag full of something called doughnuts, pastry thingies with jam inside and covered in sugar.

As she filled a kettle with water to make a cup of tea for her and the old man, I reached on to the table and hooked the bag onto the floor. These 'doughnuts' are big round things - and what do big round things do? They roll. They fell out the bag and rolled across the kitchen floor in all directions. I didn't know which one to chase first.

The old woman stepped on one and slipped onto her backside. The old man ran to help, skidded in a puddle of jam and fell over the old woman. They both sat on the floor, glaring at me.

The old man stood up and tried to wipe the jam off his trousers but only succeeded in smearing it over a greater area.

'Toffee, Toffee, you, you, you...BAD GIRL!' spluttered the old woman.

What! Bad? I've stopped you from snaffling a teeth-rotting, diabetes-inducing, weight-gaining lump of empty calories – and I'm BAD?

I held my tail high in the air and stalked out.

There's just no pleasing some people.

June 8

What Cat wants, Cat gets.

On a completely unrelated matter, the old man is saying to the old woman, 'Did we eat all that Brie? I thought there was quite a bit left.'

June 9

The old man spent all evening with his earphones on listening to some band called Led Zeppelin. Stupid name. What does it even mean?

Every so often he'd pull one earphone from his ear and shout things like, 'I BLOODY LOVE STAIRWAY TO HEAVEN, DON'T YOU?' or he'd start singing along which caused the old woman to poke him in the ribs.

'ISN'T THIS THE BEST THING IN THE WORLD!' he shouted at one point.

The old woman and I looked at each other. No it isn't. Best thing? I could tell she was thinking about chocolate cake - and I was thinking about wrapping up Rajah/Percy and posting him to Timbuctoo.

June 10

The old man and the old woman went off to a party this evening. It was fancy dress on the theme of superheroes.

The old man came down the stairs wearing a black cape and some weird hood with ears. He was singing da da da da da da da da BATMAN! The old woman had also opted for a hood with pointy ears, plus black tights, black top and a thick leather belt. She meowed and clawed at the air and announced she was Cat Woman.

Holy nightmare. Batman and Cat Woman? They looked more like Laurel and Hardy on a bad day.

Their capes were so synthetic I was praying they didn't go near a naked flame or they would go up like a bush fire.

But they seemed to enjoy themselves. The two of them fell out of a taxi in the early hours of the morning and rolled into the house a bit wobbly and giggly. The old man made a beeline for me but I skedaddled up the stairs to the spare bedroom.

Oh my stars and garters, I'm keeping out of their way until Batman and Cat Woman have reverted to being the boring old man and old woman..

June 11

I am suffering from insomnia. I have slept only 17hrs and 55mins today instead of my customary 18hrs.

Tired.

June 12

I have to report the old man is very ill (making a fuss about nothing) and is suffering from horrendous flu (slight sniffle) but he's being very heroic (crying like a baby) and isn't making a fuss at all (has the old woman running around like a blue-arsed fly). He's struggled off to work (hooray!) because he's such a brave little soldier (the old woman might have to shoot him later).

June 13

The old woman was reading an article about cat horoscopes. It seems I am a Leo. Leo the Lion. I'm not surprised.

'Leo cats are domineering,' she read. Of course. 'They are full of their own superiority, believing themselves to be ruler of all they survey.' Naturally. 'They think they are highly intelligent.' No 'thinks' about it. I am. 'They have a commanding presence and stately bearing.' I do. I really do.

'The Leo cats' homes are their castle and they consider themselves the monarch. Their owners are there to serve them.' There's a mistake in this. I own the old man and the old woman, not the other way around.

'They have to be the centre of attention.' I always am. 'They don't suffer fools gladly.' I don't. 'They demand the top quality in everything - food, toys, beds - as befits their royal status.' Chance would be a fine thing.

'If you keep them happy they will be loyal, loving and the ideal pet.'

Couldn't have put it better myself.

June 14

This afternoon I walked across the keyboard of the old woman's laptop. I think she's going to love that original painting of an armadillo dressed as Napoleon that I've ordered for her.

June 15

Today I learned that yowling at a packet of prawns will not make it open by itself.

June 16

I've decided today is Pamper Your Cat Day. How can I communicate this to the old man and the old woman?

It's now 10pm and I'm sad to report that not one iota of pampering has been in evidence, apart from feeding on demand and some heavy duty grooming with my favourite soft brush.

I feel neglected…and not a little sad.

June 17

The old woman was on the laptop looking for a new T-shirt.

'Look at this!' she said to the old man. 'Isn't it cute?'

She showed him a T-shirt for sale with the slogan, 'Cats leave pawprints on your heart.'

The old man said: 'Yeah, and on floors you've just washed, all over the furniture, on windowsills, on clean bedding, on your new white shirt (while you're wearing it), in wet cement, on clean cars, on neatly folded piles of fresh laundry...'

Unnecessary, I thought.

June 18

4am is the best time of the day. Judging by their annoyed and bleary expressions, the old man and the old woman do not agree.

June 19

I overheard the old woman telling the old man that one of her work colleagues didn't like cats. He looked at her in horror.

'I know!' she said, shocked. 'Either you're a cat lover or you are an idiot with fewer brain cells than an amoeba.'

He nodded in agreement.

Aw, you guys!

June 20

I am uniquely placed to share my views on the advantages of older pets as I live with two hoomans who won't see 40 again.

For those of you who are unsure about adopting an older person, there is information on the Cats Protection website in a post called The Adult Advantage. They seem to have mistakenly used the word 'cat' instead of 'person' and included other little typos like saying 'litterbox' instead of toilet so I have corrected these for you. You're welcome.

So here it is:

1. An adult person's personality has already developed, so you'll know if he or she is a good fit for your family.

2. An adult person may very well already know basic household etiquette (like not attacking your feet at night). In particu-

lar, senior people are often already house trained and are less likely to 'forget' where the toilet is.

3. An adult person won't grow any larger - well, as long as it doesn't eat too much! - so you'll know exactly how much person you're getting.

4. Adult people are often content to just relax in your company, unlike younger people, who may get into mischief because they're bored. Adult people also make great napping partners!

5. Adult people have often already been taught that scratching posts (not furniture) are for scratching and toys (not hands or feet) are for biting.

6. Adult people are harder to find homes for, and generally the older the person, the harder it is to rehome. When you adopt a senior person, you're truly saving a life.

How nice to know I am saving the lives of the old man and the old woman.

June 21

Rajah/Percy slipped into my garden. He didn't realise I was under the bush. I leapt up, yowling and scared the bejesus out of him. Today has all the makings of a GOOD day.

June 22

Take a chill pill, old woman. Just because I accidentally knocked a cup of steaming hot tea into your briefcase containing lots of 'precious things' (as if...), including your diary, work papers and that 5,000 word report for the boss you were sweating over for a week, there's no need to get quite so upset.

Such a drama queen.

June 23

Someone's left the milk out. Thirsty. Oh dear, it seems to have fallen all by itself to the floor. Big puddle. It looks so yellow and creamy.

BLEUCH! Who puts banana in milk? Who? Who?

June 24

Oh no, oh no, oh no, oh no.

The old woman had decided, as she does periodically, to get fit. She's been trawling the internet looking for tips and miracle products that will make her lose three stone without having to change her lifestyle one iota. Having decided that this is impossible, she has been researching diet and exercise programmes.

None of that should concern me, except she has the tendency to throw herself whole-heartedly into these projects. Hence, she's forever watching keep-fit DVDs and leaping about the sitting-room, disturbing my rest.

Or she's in the kitchen cooking up some vile smelling concoction full of things like kale, quinoa and boiled wheat grass. Then there are all those fat-free, taste-free quorn products. Quorn. The spawn of the devil. It looks like meat but is made of fungus. The only good thing about it is that it's marginally better than tofu.

All very distressing to a confirmed carnivore like me.

The old man and I have been keeping out of her way. At the moment we are curled up on the bed. He's eating peanuts while feeding me chicken flavour cat treats. From the sitting-room below we can hear dance music, and a woman exhorting her class to 'lift higher' and 'double the pace'. From the sound of the bumps and banging I think a herd of elephants has decided to pay us a visit.

I'm staying put. The old man looks at me.

'TV, I think, Toffee,' he says as he switches on a football match at maximum volume. I sigh and settle down for a nap.

June 25

Maybe I shouldn't have attacked the sofa but I'm too beautiful to feel shame.

June 26

It was raining last night. I went out hunting and caught myself a lovely little mouse. We played for a bit, you know how it is, before he hitched a ride in my mouth and we went inside.

I was feeling generous and thought I'd share the *lurve* so I

78

pushed open the bedroom door, went to the old woman's side of the bed and crawled under the duvet, snuggling up to her stomach, thinking I'd soon get dry.

She woke up with a start, screamed and accidentally hit the old man in the face. That scream was just a starter. You should have heard her screeching when she felt the mouse rushing about under the duvet trying to escape.

It was half an hour before they managed to catch it. And then what did they do? You're hardly going to believe this. They took my precious gift and let it go in the garden.

As for me, I've been imprisoned in the spare bedroom with no immediate prospect of parole. They are deaf to my scratching and meowing.

You *try* to be generous and that's all the thanks you get.

June 27

The old woman had one of her dopey work friends over for lunch. They were wittering away with their glasses of red wine and bowl of spaghetti bolognese. I spotted Mr Fluffy Bum on the other side of the kitchen and ran full pelt across the table.

There was no need to use that language, old woman. I had NO IDEA that my actions would ruin your lunch.

She seemed to be in a bit of a bad mood for the rest of the day. When she fed me in the evening I turned my nose up at the chicken in gravy in my bowl.

The old woman was cross. "Really, Toffee, how hungry are you if you won't eat perfectly good cat food?" Hungry enough to want POSH food from tin foil trays not out of bog standard pouches. Look at the adverts. The food is in TERRINE. TERRINE. I don't know what terrine is but even so, TERRINE. Shape up, old woman.

June 28

The old woman today decided to take up something called Knitting. The Old Man looked at her dubiously.

'I didn't know you could knit,' he said.

'Of course I can knit. I learned to knit at school. I was good at knitting,' she replied.

'I've never seen you knit. Are you sure you can remember how?'

She sighed, deeply. 'Of course I can *remember*. It's like riding a bike, you never forget.'

'Like you *remembered* when we were on holiday and you fell off into that steaming pile of cow shit, you mean?'

She stared him for a good five seconds. Oo, I thought. He's getting the look.

He quickly buried his head in his newspaper.

I fell asleep but awoke to the sound of click-clack-click-clack-pause-click-click-pause-click-longer pause-click-clack. I opened one eye and there was the old woman on the sofa beside me holding Long Pointy Sticks with wool wrapped around them. And there on the floor was Ball Of Wool. Let me at it!

I jumped to the floor and attacked Ball Of Wool.

'No, Toffee,' the old woman shouted. 'Leave it alone.' She picked up Ball Of Wool and put it under the cushion beside her.

I returned to the sofa and started to bat at Pointy Sticks.

'Toffee, for goodness sake, stop it!'

She picked me up and carried me to the kitchen and put some food in the bowl. She shut me out of the sitting-room but even through a thick wooden door all I could hear was an infernal click-clacking that went on all evening.

I don't think I can bear it much longer.

June 29

The Knitting continues. There is now about two inches of knitted fabric. This, she told the old man, is The Rib. There are also a couple of holes where she has done something which I believe is called Dropping A Stitch.

'What on earth is it going to be?' asked The Old Man.

'Isn't it obvious? It's this,' and she thrust Knitting Pattern into his hand. He began to laugh loudly.

'Oh my! Lucky old Toffee!' he spluttered.

The old woman frowned.

80

'Will you shut up and stop being so stupid. I need to get on with it.'

Lucky old Toffee? What did that mean?

I looked at the pattern. There was the picture of a cat being tortured. Yes, tortured. There is no other word for it. Poor puss had been forced to wear a baby pink jumper covered in pale blue pom-poms.

She doesn't seriously think that thing is getting within 20 yards of my body, does she?

June 30

Tonight as the old man and the old woman slept I wreaked havoc on Ball Of Wool. He now lies unravelled and in tatters throughout the sitting-room, hall and kitchen. I have chewed Long Pointy Sticks and I have put even more holes in The Rib. Knitting Pattern lies in tatters.

When the old woman got up this morning I was hiding behind the sofa. She yelled. She yelled very loudly.

The old man came down. He laughed. He laughed very loudly.

She sighed. She sighed very crossly and deeply.

The old man gathered up all the bits from the instrument of torture and flung them into the bin.

There will be no more Knitting.

JULY

July 1

Non, rien de rien, non, je ne regrette rien.

Which, I think, loosely translated means 'up yours;.

July 2

The old woman is shouting at me FOR NO REASON. I'm going to sulk while she brushes up that broken mug.

July 3

I have never been so insulted in my life. And I have been insulted plenty, I can tell you.

The old woman was again reading some darn book about cats and came up with this little snippet: 'The vast majority of cats are mongrels.'

She ruffled my ears. 'Just like you, Toffee.'

W-H-A-A-A-T? ME, A MONGREL?

How dare she say such a thing. I might not be a Persian cat or even a part-Persian cat. I'm thinking of that dipstick Rajah/Percy next door. But I am a..., a..., a..., I know, I am of the breed Superior Being.

She went on reading. She doesn't know when to stop, that woman.

'Cats have been especially bred for a variety of reasons; to produce softer or longer coats, for example, or to enhance their markings or refine a colour. In the eyes of the breeders, the refinements have enhanced their beauty.'

That did it for me. Was she implying that I was not as handsome as some Persian cat? How very, very dare she.

I leapt to my feet scrabbled across her hand, digging my claws in as I went. She shrieked and sucked on her hand.

'Pity you weren't bred to be a NICE CAT and not a monster,' she yelled after my retreating, ginger behind.

We aren't speaking to each other at the moment but I might deign to be a 'NICE CAT' when it's time for tea.

July 4

The old woman is having a go at me just because her new pot plant seems to have lost quite a few of its leaves.

Talk to the paw, lady, talk to the paw.

July 5

The weather is warm at the moment and the old man and the old woman have been dusting off the barbecue and casting wistful looks at the sausages and burgers in the deep freeze.

They are simple souls and like nothing better than cremating what was previously a perfectly good piece of meat. Still, it's often raw in the middle so I guess that evens things out.

I don't mind a barbecue because in the morning I can help with the housework by hoovering up the collateral damage of discarded meat products. Yum. I keep as far away as possible from the actual event, not least because their daft friends insist on eating to what they call 'music' and what I call 'an assault on the ears'.

The preparations drive me batty. They always have a garden makeover before inviting people to share in their culinary catastrophes. The lawnmower, buzzing like several swarms of angry bees, strips away the long grass in which I like to hide while stalking little creatures. Then there's the ear-splitting strimmer. How can I sleep with all that kerfuffle going on?

Usually these friends bring along smaller versions of themselves - 'children', I think they're called. This selection of anklebiters, horror of horrors, want to play with me. Another reason for boycotting the event and scuttling off to a hidey-hole. These 'children' scream and fight over the minuscule paddling pool the old man and the old woman bought for a pittance in a car boot sale and then had to mend with a bicycle tyre repair kit.

Hardly a brain cell between them.

When all the gardening has been done and the children at last subdued, there is that crazy summer ceremony - the lighting of said barbecue. The old man spends about half an hour holding matches to firelighters and charcoal. It smoulders for a short while, sending up clouds of smoke before he gets a fire going hot enough to just about warm through a pork chop rind. That stage lasts for half an hour before the next phase when it suddenly flares into life and becomes hot enough to strip the paint off the garage door at 20 paces.

I'll be glad when it rains again so I can pop outdoors, get soaking wet and then jump on either the old man or the old woman to get myself dry. They usually put up with me and I end up warm and cosy between them on the sofa.

They do have their uses.

July 6

It is is my day of rest. As was yesterday and the day before that and the day before. As it will be tomorrow and the day after tomorrow.

July 7

Today is the old woman's birthday. I gave her a dead mouse. She screamed with delight.

July 8

Yesterday the old man gave the old woman a new camera for her birthday. Lord. Today I've had that bloody camera in my face all day long. I wake from a sleep and she's there in front of me taking a picture. I go to my cat bowl and get blinded by the flash, I walk out through the cat flap and she's photographing my arse. There's something wrong with the woman.

Seriously.

July 9

This evening the old man took the old woman out to dinner for a belated birthday meal. I think they both enjoyed it. The old man had so much food on his tie when he got home that if you boiled it you could make soup.

July 10

The photography continues. The old woman's Facebook page is awash with photos. There's one of last night's dinner, one of the only shrub in the garden that isn't half dead, another of the old man holding up a glass of wine, a selfie of the two of them grinning into the camera like two mad loons.

They've all got comments from her friends like, 'Lovely pic, babe,' 'Aw, you two!', 'Looks delish, hun,' and 'Well done you!'

Today she posted one of my rear end filling up the cat flap as I exited the house. I couldn't believe an earlier one of me posing like the feline goddess I am got 30 likes and this one got 121.

WHAT IS THE MATTER WITH YOU FACEBOOK PEOPLE?

July 11

The old woman is still wandering around with that bloody camera in her hand. She walks into the sitting-room and the old man puts up his hands. 'Don't shoot!' he says.

'I don't want a picture of you, I want one of our gorgeous Toffee.'

She might be annoying but at least she's not stupid.

July 12

I was sleeping peacefully in the middle of the night when I was awoken by the old man shouting loud enough to wake the dead. Appears he'd got up in the dark to go the loo and trodden on toys 'someone' had left on the landing.

It's his own fault, he shouldn't have drunk that mug of tea just before going to bed.

July 13

What do you mean, there was no Cattalicious Chunky Rabbit in the supermarket? Go to another one, don't feed me this second grade gloop.

July 14

There I was minding my own business having a brief nap on the sofa when the old woman crept up on me.

'You're mad,' said the old man 'She'll never go for it.'

'Course she will, she'll love it!' said the old woman.

I heard what they were saying but couldn't be bothered to open my eyes as I assumed they were talking about one of their dimwit relations, probably that niece with the weird offspring.

Suddenly, I felt something being put over my head and around my chest.

What fresh torture was this?

I leapt to my feet, looked down over myself and realised I had been trussed like a chicken in some ill-fitting harness contraption with a lead attached.

'Come on,' said the old woman brightly. 'We're going for a walk.'

WHAT!

YOU might be going for a walk, missus, I certainly am not.

She lifted me up and carried me outside. She put me down and gave a little tug to the leash. With admirable restraint I refrained from attacking her legs.

'Come on Toffee, walkies!' I walked onto the grass. She tried to pull me forward. I lay down. She dragged me along the lawn.

'Toffee, stand up. We're going for a walk.'

I dug my claws into the grass. She tugged harder and dragged me a bit further. I made a run for it, taking her by surprise, and scaled the nearest tree, the harness trailing behind me.

She stood underneath, calling me.

'Come down, Toffee. It's OK. You don't have to go for a walk. I'll get you some prawns. Don't stay up there, you might get the lead tangled in the branches.'

The old man, who had been watching from the doorway, reached up, lifted me from the tree and removed the harness. He appeared to be laughing about something. Not sure what.

'That went well!' he said to the old woman.

She stared at him, stony-faced, snatched the harness and stalked off indoors.

The old man tickled me under the chin.

'Come on, girl. Let's go find some prawns.'

July 15

I fear I do not sufficiently understand the hooman race. In an effort to get into the head of the old woman. I sat on her chest in bed and stared. She awoke and pushed me off. When she fell back asleep I sat on her chest again and resumed my staring. This happened five or six times until the alarm went off.

'I've hardly slept a wink,' she told the old man. 'That cat's been creeping me out.'

'The staring?' he asked. She nodded.

'I know,' he replied. 'Sometimes she's like someone out of Nightmare On Elm Street.'

Nightmare On Elm Street? I don't remember seeing a beautiful ginger cat in that. I thought I was more like the cat in the old Disney film The Three Lives of Thomasina, based on the Paul Gallico book Thomasina: The Cat Who Thought She Was God.

Oh, that's a good idea for a film. Toffee: The Cat Who WAS God.

Take note, Disney.

July 16

Tonight the old woman went out for a drink with the 'girls' from work. She calls them 'girls' but there's not one of them under 30. In fact, I sometimes think there's not one of them under 30 stone.

She got home a little the worse for wear and proceeded to demonstrate twerking to the old man. She looked like she'd put two angry ferrets down the back of her knickers.

Not a pretty sight.

July 17

I am persona non grata yet again, just because hoomans are not clever enough to learn cat language.

Unfortunately, evolution has not arranged it so we cats have moveable mouth parts and a suitable larynx to talk to hoomans so we have found other ways to let them know what we want.

Some of these ways, I concede, hoomans can find annoying but what's a cat to do? The methods include persistent meowing, throwing up and pressing our heads into faces.

Today I employed the tactic of weaving in and out of hooman legs to draw attention to the fact that my food bowl was empty. The old man now has a bruise the size of China on his behind after falling arse over tit and I have been banished to the utility room.

Unfair. It's not my fault you hoomans have only two legs and are not as stable as we quadrupeds.

July 18

The old woman wasn't working today and decided she was going to get to grips with cleaning the house. Out came all the sprays, cloths and brushes. On went the apron and on went the rubber gloves.

Off came the rubber gloves.

'I'd better be organised and make a list first,' she said to me. I hope 'prawns for Toffee' is item number one.

She wrote the list while drinking a cup of coffee and eating biscuits. She piled dirty dishes into the dishwasher and clothes into the washing-machine. I followed her into the sitting-room where she started dusting and polishing. She sat down on the sofa to polish the coffee table. While there she switched on the tellybox and ended up watching two back-to-back episodes of Friends while drinking more coffee and eating more biscuits.

I followed her upstairs. In the bedroom she very kindly put on a new duvet cover for me to lie on. I half slept as she tidied and polished the bedroom. Dusting her bedside table she picked up a book and flicked through it. She sat on the bed and started reading it. Then she lay on the bed. Another hour later and it was lunchtime for both of us. She ate hers while watching an old black and white film on the tellybox.

After lunch she removed clothes from the washing-machine and piled in another load picked up from the bedroom floor. Then it was back upstairs to the spare bedroom to tackle a pile of magazines.

She flicked through one.

'Oh look, Toffee, there's an article here about what to buy

your cat for Christmas.'

Another article caught her eye. And another. And another.

Then came the sound of the front door opening. She leapt to her feet and start feverishly sorting through the pile of magazines. The old man poked his head around the bedroom door. 'You're busy!" he says.

She rubbed the back of her hand across her forehead and sighed deeply.

'I should say, but if it's got to be done, it's got to be done,' she said.

'Tell you what, darling, you have a rest while I cook the tea.'

'That would be wonderful.'

And she didn't even have the grace to sound the teeniest bit guilty.

July 19

Yesterday I resolved to be less clumsy after getting into trouble for smashing a glass bowl as I slid across the table to reach some prawns. Today I broke my resolution. I also broke a cup, a saucer and a wooden toy the old woman had bought for Violet's Little Person.

July 20

Today I am being rather less energetic and have decided to watch the world go by sitting in the sun on the windowsill.

Zzzzzzzz.

July 21

Busy night herding socks. They're all in a pile in the garden.

July 22

What circle of hell is this? I am sitting under the coffee table while a demented servant of Satan whirls about snuffling and snapping. I swiped his nose when he poked it under the table and he made a yelping noise and backed off. I'm safe for now, but will he and other minions of Beelzebub return to torment me?

The old man and the old woman have betrayed me. In an act of treachery that is hard to fathom, they let this slobbering beast into the house with his hooman disciple.

'He's very well behaved,' said Disciple. She lied.

I learned that this beast is called, 'Sit!' because that is what she keeps shouting at him.

Sit is now clawing at the old man's leg. I can see the old man is less than pleased. He has that smile/grimace/Bugger-OffYouLittleShit look on his face.

'He's only playing!' Disciple says brightly.

The old man tries to sound jokey but I can tell he means every word; jaw is clenched, teeth don't part. 'Well, let him play with someone else then.' Disciple laughs.

The old woman looks worried. She glances at me and then at the old man's clawed trousers.

'Let him come into the kitchen with me,' she says, 'I think there's a little bit of beef in the fridge. Would he like that?'

'Would you, boy? Would you? Would you? Yes, you would. Yes, you would. Yes, you would. Say thank you. Go on, say thank you. Say, thank you,' says Disciple, in that talking to a dim child voice.

Sit stares at her, as well he might; she is obviously completely bonkers. And he is obviously a pouch of meaty chunks short of a box if he has to have everything repeated three times.

The old woman takes him off to the kitchen, shutting the door firmly behind her. She returns alone. I'm hoping she has consigned him from whence he came. If the consigning involved red hot needles and a ramrod, so much the better.

'I've made a pot of tea and some sandwiches,' she says, 'so if you'd like to come through...' They all disappear. I stay under the table until I hear the front door close. I emerge from under the coffee table as the old man and the old woman come back into the room.

'Thank God she's gone,' says the old man, flopping onto to the sofa. I climb up beside him and he absent-mindedly strokes my ears. 'I don't know who's more annoying that woman or the bloody dog.'

Dog? Was it a dog? I suppose that's marginally better than a servant of Satan. Only marginally.

July 23

I was in the garden in the early hours of the morning, surveying my territory, when I came across a dead grass snake.

I could have stayed and played with it but, no, generous kitty that I am, I decided to make a present of it for the old man and the old woman. And, let me tell you, it wasn't easy dragging that long slippery thing through the cat flap and into the house. I pulled it through the house, up the stairs and into the bedroom where both were sleeping. I put it on the pillow between them and settled back to watch their response when they awoke. The old woman was so excited she screeched. The old man, however, didn't seem to like the gift - and was so rude he didn't even try to hide his dislike. He yelled, 'What the... [insert VERY rude word],' picked it up by its tail and threw it out of the window.

Ingrate.

July 24

Contrary to popular opinion I am not a lazy git who snoozes and potters all day. I have hobbies. Today, for example, I pursued my hobby of hunting. No guns were involved, only razor-sharp teeth and claws.

It wasn't a particularly successful day, my only 'kills' being two spiders, a beetle, and a small cardboard box which was blowing about the garden. I mistook it for an evil ninja intent on destroying the world. It is now an ex-cardboard box. It has been repurposed into mulch.

I also fish - in next door's pond. They are not best pleased. I surf the net for hilarious cat videos when the laptop is left on - some of those guys just crack me up! And, as I have mentioned before, I practise the art of contemplative yoga (i.e sleeping).

Even though my days are pretty full I am considering taking up a new hobby to while away those long afternoons when the old man and the old woman are at work.

Thinking.... zzzzzzzz.

July 25

The old woman is cross. I have shredded one of her scarves.

She should be grateful. It was hideous.

July 26

The old man and the old woman have thoughtfully provided me with several new 'beds'. They have lids that close and are full of soft clothes. I heard the old man call them 'suitcases'.

July 27

I'm worried. I think the old man and the old woman have been kidnapped. I haven't seen them all day.

July 28

There was no sighting of the old man and the old woman at all yesterday but the old woman's niece Cleo arrived in the afternoon. I have at least been fed. She spent all evening on her mobile phone. I wonder if she is negotiating with kidnappers? If she is, one of them is called Babe.

July 29

Cleo has gone and her place has been taken by her sister Clementine. She fed me, stroked me and said, 'Don't worry, Toffee, they'll be back from holiday soon.'

HOLIDAY? That treacherous pair.

July 30

I am pissed off, well and truly pissed off.

I have been abandoned and I can't remember the telephone number for Cats Protection.

July 31

The old man and the old woman have left me Home Alone, like some feline Macauley Culkin, Yes, ALONE.

Well, nearly alone. Apart from Clementine and Cleo who have taken it in turns to pop in regularly to make sure I am fed, watered and unkidnapped. They have checked I haven't been sold to a ginger-slave trader and forced to sleep in a cold and cheerless attic, eat cheap supermarket own brand slop and made to keep down the mice population of a small town.

Admittedly, they have taken it in turns to stay the night so in fact I have had more company than I do when the old man and the old woman are both working. BUT THAT'S NOT THE POINT.

How could the dastardly duo so callously abandon me to my fate?

The two girls are fine in their own way but they don't know me as well as the old man and the old woman do so are neglectful in certain areas. I tried to show my displeasure by sitting on top of the bookcase and giving Girl One the evil eye. She didn't even notice and I couldn't stay up there long as a cat's gotta eat and she had just filled my bowl with tuna chunks.

I surprised Girl Two with the 'gift' of a mouse but all she did was scream like... well, like a girl, and got out the rubber gloves to dispose of it.

Neither of them know even the most basic cat care. Can you believe it, they didn't even have the rudimentary skill of ear-rubbing. I KNOW! Astonishing in this day and age. In fact my ears were badly neglected receiving only a cursory stroke as the hand travelled from head to tail. They have not mastered the art of stretching out on the sofa so I can sit on their legs. In fact, not once did either of them put their feet up.

*shakes head in bewilderment

Both of them shut the bedroom against me, leaving me outside to make my displeasure known vociferously until they opened it and I stalked in with my tail held high to take my rightful place on the duvet.

Amateurs, the pair of them.

AUGUST

August 1

The old man and the old woman have returned. They tried to make an almighty great fuss of me but I was having none of it. I gave them my most disdainful look and stalked off to sleep in the garden. They brought me lots of presents so when I felt I had punished them for long enough, I came back in to rip off paper, chew treats and play with feathery things.

The old woman is now singing as loudly and tunelessly as ever in the kitchen and the old man is stretched out on the sofa with the tellybox remote welded to his hand and me under his chin.

At 10pm he says to the old woman, 'Can you take Toffee? My bladder is approaching critical mass.'

At last, normal service has been resumed.

August 2

I have mentioned before about my ability to take over a bed. The old man and the old woman believe the bed belongs to them. They are wrong. The bed belongs to me.

I allow them to sleep there because I am a magnanimous moggie, full of the milk of feline kindness. But I do like to have plenty of ROOOOOOM. Some mornings as I stretch across the bed to my full length I can hear them muttering as they perch precariously on the edge.

'How does she do it?'

'How can something so little take up so much room?'

'I'm practically falling off the side of the bed.'

I can hear you asking why they don't just shut me out of the bedroom. They have tried but the scratches on the door do not sit well their idea of interior design ... apparently. And I have perfected this 'poor pussycat being strangled' meow which is enough to wake the dead, let alone two moderately light sleepers.

So I stake my claim every night. I don't always take up all the bed, sometimes I save space by sitting on the old man's head or the old woman's chest. Often, I don't even sleep on the bed at all. I run about the room instead, playing with anything I can and jumping up and down off the furniture. That doesn't make them happy either, for some reason.

Anyway, it's now 8am and I have had a strenuous half hour eating breakfast and performing my morning ablutions. It's all very tiring work so please excuse me while I find a convenient place for a kip. It's clean bedding day so I think I'll settle down on the bed right in the middle of the duvet.

August 3

I am in trouble after an "incident" involving some salmon fillets and my mouth. So, in order to get back into good books, I am employing my best 'looking cute' tactics, all big eyes, paw placed gently onto hooman arms and trying to form my mouth into a smile.

'I think Toffee's got the bellyache,' said the old man.

'Serve her right for pinching that salmon,' said the old woman.

They have hearts of stone.

August 4

The old man walked in and found the old woman watching a boxing match on the tellybox.

'I didn't know you liked boxing,' said the old man.

'I don't,' she said. 'I want to watch Downton Abbey but I can't reach the remote.'

Stop talking, old woman. Your jaw is moving and disturbing my rest up here under your chin.

August 5

I tried an experiment today. I wanted to see if it was possible to tear open a pouch of meaty chunks on the sofa without getting gravy all over the cushions, floor and walls.

It isn't.

Never mind, at least I learnt a valuable lesson. If at first you don't succeed, hide the evidence.

August 6

The old man and the old woman are on the sofa watching the tellybox, drinking beer, eating kebabs and scratching their crotches.

White trash, the pair of them.

August 7

Things I have learned today:

Windows may look as if you can jump through them but you can't. Unless they're open. But usually they're shut.

Never attack a cactus before ascertaining whether there are tweezers in the house.

The stairs are not a slalom.

Feline attendance is not mandatory in the bathroom.

Oh well, you live and learn.

August 8

It has come to my attention that today is International Cat Day. So, old man and old woman, where are my gifts, my fresh prawns, my showering of attention, my adoration? Zilch, nada, nothing. Not even a defrosted prawn has been wafted past my twitching nostrils.

The tellybox was on briefly this morning and there wasn't a mention on the news. I couldn't believe it. The old man and the old woman tutted at the tales of destruction across the world and smiled at the quirky item at the end which was about some dumb dog-related video that had gone viral. Why encourage dogs to be incredibly stupid when they are managing so well on their own?

Then it was off to work. What? No time off to help me celebrate my special day?

When they came home with arms devoid of presents I finally had to concede that they had no idea of the enormity of the occasion. I sat on the armchair, my head pressed into the back and my bum towards the room.

The old man tried to pet me. I ignored him. The old woman ruffled my ears. I pulled my head away.

'What's the matter with Toffee?' said the old man. She seems a bit out of sorts.'

'She's probably just tired,' said the old woman, 'After all she's only slept for 12 hours today!' And they both started laughing.

Laugh now, you two. Revenge is a gift best served cold.

August 9

Ha, ha, ha, ha, ha! (Evil laugh.) Today I got my revenge. Forget International Cat Day, would you? Let's make today International Get Even Day, shall we?

I employed all the tools in my arsenal - sleep deprivation, inappropriate vomiting, insect infiltration, dismemberment, dematerialisation and emotional blackmail.

It all began in the witching hour in the middle of the night. I started to yowl and jump about the bedroom, knocking items off the dressing table and running up and down the two bodies in the bed. Both sat up sharply. The light went on and four sleepy eyes stared at me.

'Whaaa-t's goin' on, Toffee?' asked the old man.

The old woman, with her hair all on end and her red eyes, looked like she'd liberally applied Halloween make-up. I settled down between them and looked at them innocently as if I had been lying there all night.

The light went off and I allowed them to fall sleep before going through the procedure all over again. Then again. Then again.

By morning they *both* looked like they were ready for Halloween.

They fed me breakfast and I brought it all up again, half onto the old woman's clean jacket she had put out for work and the other half on the old man's washed and ironed white shirt.

They weren't pleased.

While they were at work I hunted in the garden for the biggest spiders I could find. I carried them in and stored them in the bathroom shower cubicle. The piercing screams from the old woman later in the day were very satisfying. Similarly the yells from the old man when he found half a mouse neatly arranged on his laptop.

Then, abracadabra, I disappeared.

They searched high and low for me. They went out into the garden and called me. They looked in every room. They moved furniture. They put fresh prawns in my bowl - that was tempting, I must admit, but I held firm.

When they reached the stage of wondering if it was appropriate to call the police to report a lost cat, I emerged from my hiding place under the clothes in the laundry basket.

The old woman swept me up in her arms. 'Toffee, we were so worried,' she said. The old man rubbed me behind the ears. 'Don't ever do that again,' he said, as he placed me beside my food bowl. That night I slept the sleep of the just, snuggled up between them.

They have learned the lesson.

August 10

Oh dear. The old man and the old woman are at war. They glare at each other over the cornflakes in the morning, and talk in clipped tones about who gets what.

We're not talking about big things like who gets custody of ME. They are talking rubbish. Yes, a big skip/dumpster stands at the side of the house in all its rusting, yellow-paint-peeling glory.

The old woman is a woman on a mission, going through drawers and cupboards and tossing away items willy-nilly. But the old man is much more restrained. He wants to assess every item. If there's the teeniest chance that he might need it in 2037 if, for example, an asteroid hits the house then he wants to be ready for it. I can hear him now, 'Bet you're glad I never let you throw away that leaking rubbish bin in 1992; see how handy it is for picking up rubble.'

If there's ever a rubber band shortage, we're prepared. Need a paperclip? We have two drawers full of them.

Today the old woman caught him leaning into the skip, his arse in the air, as he foraged around. In the end he emerged triumphant, brandishing an old tattered book, its cover warped and its pages stuck together with damp.

'You've thrown away my Boys' Own Book of Industrial Gas Mantles,' he said accusingly. The old woman walked off indoors, mumbling under her breath.

August 11

Skip wars continue.

Now they are having an argument over a broken lawnmower. 'But it's BROKEN,' the old woman yells.

'I could easily mend it,' says the old man.

'You haven't bothered in 20 years, why would you want to now?' I see a flicker in his eyes and I can see he's thinking that if he mends it, he might be expected to use it. In the end he grudgingly concedes.

The old woman has even been encouraging him to go the pub (not a difficult task) and as soon as he's out the door, she's loading up bin bags with half empty paint tins, fossilised paintbrushes, mouse-eared books and broken plant pots.

This evening I perched on top of the rubbish as the old woman carried out some ancient curtains. She lifted me off and arranged the curtains over the rubbish to hide what was underneath.

'There, Toffee,' she said. 'Out of sight, out of mind.' She paused, 'If he still insists on hoicking some mouldering decrepit item out of the skip, I'm throwing him in it. Then I'm going to stick tubes up his nose and a long nozzle up his rear end. That way, anyone glancing in will think he's an old vacuum cleaner.'

She wiped her hands down her trousers and laughed. I'm still slightly worried about the maniacal look in her eye.

Later that day the skip/dumpster was collected.

Thank heaven for that.

August 12

IT'S MY BIRTHDAY! IT'S MY BIRTHDAY! IT'S MY BIRTHDAY! PRESENTS! I'VE GOT PRESENTS!

They are all wrapped and beside my food bowl. I hardly know what to do first, eat my rabbit chunks or tear the paper. So it's gulp, tear, gulp, tear, gulp, tear while old man and the old woman watch me and laugh.

Breakfast over, I turn my full attention to the gifts. There's a stack of foil dishes of food. FOIL! FOIL! Not tins or pouches or bags. FOIL! I'm a posh-girl cat after all!

I have a fleecy blanket, a bird on a spring on a bouncy ball, some prawn-flavoured catty cookies and a new bowl with my name on.

I. AM. IN. HEAVEN.

The excitement has exhausted me so I ignore it all, curl up on my new blanket and … zzzzzzz.

August 13

Am I the only one around here who monitors the number of packets of prawns in the freezer? There are only five left.

FIVE.

#imminentstarvation

August 14

At last they have broken open one of those foil trays they bought me for my birthday – prime salmon in gourmet jelly.

I can hardly wait to get stuck in, jumping up and down and spinning around in circles – so excited.

Two mouthfuls later and I've lost interest. I wander nonchalantly into the sitting-room.

The old man and the old woman stare at each other.

'Not quite the reaction I was expecting,' said the old man.

'No, not quite,' said the old woman.

August 15

I try to look cool when the old man and the old woman present me with a new toy - but I'm excited inside. I love nothing better than chasing a tinkling ball or shredding ribbons and chewing on tassels.

When they are out - to be honest, I'm usually asleep - but when I am not you can often find me digging out one of my toys and having one of my funny five minutes.

The other day they were having a big tidy-up because the old woman's mother is due to visit. The old man looked worried as he always does when the Mother-slash-Mother-in-Law comes a-calling. I think she frightens him. She can be a bit stern.

They were gathering my toys together into a cardboard box and I heard the old man say to the old woman, 'What on earth does she do with all those toys we buy her? We've bought her hundreds over the years.'

She tilted the box and few furry mice and a half-chewed cardboard bird rolled to one side. She shrugged and carried on with the housework. I closed my eyes and started to dream about real mice and birds.

Suddenly my pleasant reverie was broken by a yell.

'TOFFEE!'

What was wrong? I thought I'd better go and see so I strolled into the living room. She had pulled out the sofa to hoover underneath and there were piles and piles of dusty cat toys.

Jeez. It's not my fault she's so rubbish at housework.

August 16

There's an air of doom hovering in the house. The Mother-slash-Mother-in-Law is here for a long weekend. If anyone can make a long weekend feel like an eternity, it's her.

She is one of those people who has that ability to hide an insult in a compliment.

As they sat eating lunch she said, 'I think you two are so wise not to be hung up on being slim.' Then she turned to old man, 'You're not fat, exactly, but you could do with being a few inches taller.' I was smiling to myself about that one, but then she said: 'Toffee is such a nice cat – to look at…' The rest of that sentence was left hanging in the air.

I think the old man and the old woman were concerned I might do something 'inappropriate', having blotted my copy-book with other visitors. I couldn't settle without being whisked up and put into another room. I only had to look as if I were unsheathing a claw and I'd suddenly be on the other side of the house.

I didn't know whether I was coming or going – although it was usually going.

August 17

This morning the Mother-slash-Mother-in-Law said, 'I don't know why you allow that cat to sleep on your bed, it's so un-hygienic.'

Unhygienic? The old man and the old woman shower daily.

'You don't know what germs she's got on her paws,' she went on and I realised she was talking about ME.

The claws came out but before I knew it I had been trans-ported from the sitting-room to the utility room.

The Mother-slash-Mother-in-Law is not as fit as she was. She said she finds her stairs tricky and is saving up for a stairlift.

The old man said, 'That's a really good idea,' and whispered to the old woman, 'If she wants to sit in an electric chair, I'll contribute.'

Later he whispered, 'How many mothers-in-law does it take to change a light bulb? Just the one. She holds it up there and waits for the world to revolve around her.'

The old woman nodded her head slowly and poured herself another glass of wine.

Good job The Mother-slash-Mother-in-Law is getting a bit deaf too.

August 18

Eyes streaming. Nose running. Gagging.

The Mother-slash-Mother-in-Law has gone home and her parting gift was aftershave for the old man and perfume for the old woman. No gift for me but the sight of her retreating back-side was gift enough.

The old man and the old woman have both plastered on their vile liquids and clouds of offensive odours fill the house. The combined smell could strip foliage.

'You smell like a tart's boudoir,' the old man told the old woman.

'And you smell like a crowd of teenage boys at an 80s disco,' she replied.

The old man coughed. 'It is a bit strong, it's true.' The old woman sneezed. 'I think I'm allergic.' He decided on a shower and the old woman had a bath, minus the usual bubbles and scented gel.

They are now almost back to normal although a faint mist of rancid pine and decaying flowers still hangs about their persons. Think I'll sleep on the sofa tonight.

August 19

'Look at this, dear, isn't it cute?' the old woman asked the old man. One of her friends had emailed her a picture of their new puppy. The little oik was shamelessly going for the 'ahhhh fac-tor' - I could tell by his wide-eyed fluffiness.

He didn't do anything for me. In my opinion the only good dog is a hot dog – without the mustard, onions and bread roll, obviously.

August 20

I knocked over a cup of coffee on the kitchen table.

The old woman was not very pleased. 'Toffee! You stupid cat!' Steady on there, old woman

I stared into her eyes with my best wide-eyed look (I learnt something from that puppy picture) and put my paw on her arm.

She rolled her eyes and sighed loudly before mopping up the mess.

Yes, lady, roll your eyes back much further and you might just possibly find your brain.

August 21

The old man and the old woman are not talking to each other. Again.

I fear it may be my fault.

It all started when I chased Rajah/Percy back into his own garden. I leapt from the fence onto a circular clothes dryer which proceeded to spin around at the rate of knots. I fell to the ground, dizzy and disorientated, but managed to get back over the fence.

As I plonked myself down in the laundry basket to recover I realised I had a pair knickers on my head. I shook them off and went to sleep.

When the old woman came home she lifted me from the basket and stared open-mouthed at the pink frilly concoction lying on top of the pile of clothes.

She lifted the article between her thumb and forefinger and marched into the sitting-room.

'What the hell is this?' she shouted at the old man, innocently reading the daily paper.

He looked up. 'I'm not Sherlock, but I'm guessing they're a pair of knickers,' he said.

'Yes, they are - but THEY'RE NOT MINE!'

Then the old man said something that sealed his fate and condemned him to a night sleeping in the spare bedroom.

'I can see that. They're far too small ...'

August 22

Knickergate continues. Today we had an interrogation that would put an SS officer to shame.

'Whose are they?'

'I've never seen them before in my life.'

'Who is she?'

'There is no "she". I told you, I know nothing about them.'

'So how did they get in our laundry basket?'

'I DON'T KNOW. They must be yours.'

'Oh, really? These tiny little frillies that are patently TOO

SMALL FOR ME?'

'I didn't mean you were fat...' Even I gulped at that remark.

She threw a wet dishcloth at his head and walked out.

The crest-fallen old man spent the evening alone, sitting at the kitchen table.

August 23

I can't live in this chilly atmosphere. I must do something about it. I waited until the old man and the old woman were both in the kitchen, sitting in silence at opposite ends of the table. I jumped over the fence, leapt onto the rotary dryer and pulled a pair of man's underpants from the line.

Then I dragged them back through the cat flap with a clatter.

The old man and the old woman both looked at me. The old man retrieved the underpants from my grip.

'Toffee?' said the old woman.

'What the...?' said the old man.

'Darling,' said the old woman.

'It's all right, sweetheart,' said the old man, and the soppy pair were in each other's arms.

It was only 7 o'clock but they set off for one of their 'early nights', leaving me with an empty food bowl in the kitchen.

So, that's all the gratitude I get for saving a marriage, is it?

August 24

Toast for the old man and the old woman's breakfast. She got up to switch on the radio. Quick lick.

AAAAARRRRGGGGGHHHH!

What in the name of all that's holy is that black stuff? Marmite? Who eats that? Seriously, who eats that?

August 25

Today I have been perfecting The Stare. Sadly the old man and the old woman are decidedly slow when it comes to reading my facial expressions. But I'm getting The Stare down to a fine art - even Mr and Mrs Dim won't be able to mistake my intentions.

If they feed me and I look into the bowl and give them The Stare they should jolly well know that I am less than enamoured with its contents. If I empty the bowl and give them The Stare, I am still STARVING.

If they are sitting on the sofa and reading a newspaper or a book and I jump onto their lap, claw away said publication and give them The Stare, they must immediately put aside their reading matter and give me their full attention.

If I sit in front of a door staring at it with my nose one inch away, that door MUST BE OPENED IMMEDIATELY. Similarly, if I give The Stare to cupboards or drawers, there is something inside that I want.

Come on, guys, it's not rocket science.

August 26

I am reliably informed that today is International Dog Day. Dog Day, I ask you.

Shocked and disgusted.

August 27

There's a packet of prawns missing from the table. And guess who's getting the blame as per usual? The old woman is ranting on and the old man is saying she shouldn't have left them out and now he's getting an earful.

'We can't trust you for ONE MINUTE, can we, Toffee?'

Not my problem you have trust issues.

'I needed those prawns for tea, now what are we going to do?'

Get a takeaway?

'If you've eaten them all you'll BURST, then what will you do?'

Well, not much if I've burst.

The old man takes one of my meaty pouches from the cupboard.

'PUT THAT BACK! Don't feed the little devil, she must be stuffed to the gills.'

The old man returns the pouch to its box.

'Sorry, girl,' he whispers.

That's OK, I've already had my tea.

*licks lips.

Yum, prawny.

August 28

The old woman's current favourite cookery programme is something called The Hairy Bikers. I thought it would feature cats cooking up dishes featuring prawns, tuna and rabbit. But, no. They are a pair of bearded men with strange accents who ride about on motorbikes, sampling the cuisine in various parts of the world.

She loves cookery programmes and avidly watches all the Masterchef shows and the programmes with celebrity chefs showing off their skills.

The other night she was watching a chef cook up a 'tasting menu' which included small portions of several dishes, designed to show off his repertoire.

'Oh,' she said to the old man, 'I think I'll give that a go - try out lots of new things.'

A look of horror passed over his face.

'But, but, I like your ordinary dishes. Just one at a time.'

But she was off to the kitchen to look in her cookery books. The old man stroked my head.

'Oh dear, Toffee,' he said. 'One course is usually bad enough, but several?' and sighed deeply.

Mercifully for the old man, the old woman didn't have enough ingredients for a tasting menu and knowing her she will have forgotten all about it by tomorrow.

Brain the size of a pea, even if it is a pea cooked four ways.

August 29

I spent most of the night out stalking and hunting. Quite successful too. It started to rain so I went home. I crept into bed at 2am and made the astonishing discovery that not everyone likes wet decapitated mice.

August 30

The old man and the old woman threw my best cardboard box into the rubbish bin. I was FURIOUS. It was comfy, smelled delightfully of week-old casseroled chicken and still had several square inches of unscratched surface.

By bedtime I was pacing the floor and staring meaningfully in the direction of the bin. The stupid pair were oblivious.

But as I watched them climb the stairs to go to bed I remembered the old saying, 'Never let the sun go down on your wrath.'

No, stay up and get your revenge.

Sooo, old man and old woman. Did you like the little squeaking present I left under the bed. Didcha? Didcha?

August 31

I never make mistakes. The old man and the old woman, may THINK I have made a mistake but they are wrong.

They may see me climb to the top of the bookcase and then, apparently, miss my footing and plummet to the floor. I have, however, done this completely on purpose. I am in training for the Purrlympics. Never heard of them? Well, we cats don't like to brag about our athletic expertise but we hold several events every year. I am the world champion in the Three Metre Drop and aim to keep my title this year.

The old man and the old woman may think my head is stuck in a cardboard box. No, it is not. I can remove the box whenever I like. I am just in here checking there are no insects stuck in the corners. It might take me some time. Yes, I'm still looking. I know it's been ten minutes but I am nothing if not thorough. If you want to, you can take the box off me. I will humour you and allow you to do that. Like, now? NOW!

One day the silly pair thought I had swallowed a bee by accident. Hadn't they heard that bee venom cures arthritis? I know my face blew up like a balloon and they had to take me to the vet but that's a small price to pay for not having this debilitating illness. I am aware I don't actually have arthritis but this is merely proof that my preventative measure is working.

They laugh when I apparently chase my own tail in the mistaken belief it belongs to someone else. But what I am actually doing is testing Dizziness Resistance. I must make sure that after four or five head-spinning turns I can still stand up. I am

doing this for YOU, old man and old woman. What if, for example, I spotted a mouse inside a-a-a spinning thing, how could
I rescue you from the little monster if I were having a dizzy
spell? So, you see, I am doing it all for you.

A little gratitude wouldn't go amiss.

SEPTEMBER

September 1

The old woman has a headache – she claims it's nothing to do with last night's girls' night out when she rolled home in a taxi at 2am, making enough noise to wake the dead.

She said, 'I must be sickening for something,' as the old man rolled his eyes but was wise enough to keep his mouth firmly shut.

She hunted high and low for paracetamol but couldn't find any. Fortunately she did find that tried and tested cure for headaches – a cup of tea and a packet of biscuits.

She's now spark out on the sofa snoring louder than a pneumatic drill.

September 2

The old man and the old woman are getting on a bit so have not succumbed to the fashion for tattoos – thank goodness. It would take a drawing the size of Texas to make any impression on their expanse of skin.

If they wanted to get the Complete Works of Shakespeare tattooed on their behinds, there'd be plenty of room.

Personally, I don't pay much attention. Who needs a tattoo when you are covered in spectacular ginger fur?

But the old man and the old woman have many young relatives who visit the house and lots of them have a tattoo somewhere. The old man and the old woman admire them politely but I can tell they don't really approve.

Today, though, the old woman's niece Clementine came a-calling. She rolled up her sleeve and displayed a tattoo of a ginger cat. She has taste, that girl.

'It's Toffee!' said the old woman.

Clementine frowned. 'Well, no. It's supposed to be Garfield.'

Scrub that comment about her having taste.

The girl's a nincompoop.

September 3

Today I have learned that necklaces make good toys, especially if they are made of beads and you play with them on a tiled floor. Then when the string breaks, it is interesting to see how far they roll, over how great a distance and what speed.

Educational.

September 4 (morning)

I have some sad news to impart.

I'm leaving home.

The tragic chain of events began this morning when the old man and the old woman overslept. It was nothing to do with me running around the bedroom, knocking items one by one off the dressing-table in the middle of the night, I'm sure, but because they stayed up too late watching some stupid film on the tellybox.

In their rush to get to work on time the old woman grabbed cat food from the cupboard of a brand that I had previously rejected. I cannot tolerate such treatment. I shall leave home later after I have nibbled just enough of my stockpile of bugs to save me from death by starvation.

I shall need my strength to find a new home with people who appreciate my high standards and who will not try to feed me POISON.

Goodbye, cruel people. I am off to pastures new.

After I have eaten a few more bugs.

After I have had a snooze.

After I have chased birds in the garden.

After I have played with Mr Fluffy Bum.

… I might leave it until tomorrow now.

September 4 (evening)

When the old man and the old woman came home from work,

the old man picked up the empty pouch of Vile Concoction and gasped.

'You didn't …?' he said. 'You know what happened before when I tried to feed her this rubbish.'

'Oh no, I must have used it by accident,' said the old woman.

'I thought we'd thrown it out,' said the old man.

'I was saving it, you know, just in case of a breakdown in society or something.'

'She still wouldn't eat it.'

'I know, but *we* might be forced to if we ran out of food.'

The old man took a bag of prawns from the fridge.

'There's nothing else for it.'

'I suppose not,' said the old woman.

As the old woman emptied my bowl and rinsed it out, The old man fetched scissors to open the packet the prawns and then proceeded to pour a big pile into the dish.

I will reconsider my plan to leave home. I'm too full to think about it at the moment.

September 5

Yes, I'm still here. I decided against leaving home. I am giving the old man and the old woman a second chance because I am such a kind and sensitive cat…and because they gave me prawns…and because I fell asleep and didn't wake up until it was dark and really couldn't be bothered.

Just to show I have forgiven them, I have been helping with the housework today.

I started in the sitting-room. I had a quick swish round with my paws, cleaning dust off the shelves - plus books and a stack of DVDs (I know, who still has stacks of DVDs? The old man and old woman think they live in the Middle Ages when it's just that they *are* middle-aged).

Then there was a tidy round in the kitchen. I cleared off the counters. That was easy although I must admit the broken packet of flour on the floor looks a tad untidy. Still, there's plenty of worktop space now.

Into the bedroom and I thought I'd iron out the duvet by using the heat of my body. Yes, I lay on it and it was soft, so so soft ... zzzzz.

I was awoken a few hours later by the old woman shouting, 'WHAT HAVE YOU DONE, TOFFEE?'

I thought she'd be pleased.

Nope.

September 6

I puked up the biggest hairball you've ever seen. Pity the old woman didn't spot it before she sat down.

Squelchy.

September 7

Some DOOFUS has invented a collar that can 'translate' cat meows into words. I occasionally have communication problems with the old man and the old woman, mostly because they're not very bright. Even so, I carry on long conversations with them both. In fact, sometimes when I am in the kitchen with the old woman discussing the merits of meaty chunks in gravy versus fish pate, The old man will shout from the sitting-room, 'Who are you talking to?' She replies, 'Toffee!' and he doesn't bat an eyelid.

September 8

I am once again in the old woman's bad books. She cooked a spaghetti bolognese but when she came to drain the spaghetti she found me on the kitchen worktop curled up in the colander.

She's now scrubbing it in soapy water.

There's really no need, I'm as clean as a whistle.

#whatisherproblem

September 9

Can't move. I have eaten my body weight in prawns.

September 10

What do you see when you look in the mirror? I see somebody alluring, charming, witty and erudite (I must be to use words like that) - a cat of the world. Colour: ginger. Temperament: mercurial. Character: modest. I could go on but that's all I can be bothered to say at the moment.

I'm off to sleep in my favourite spot - on top of the clean and ironed laundry in the basket; I just love the frantic running around in the morning as the old man and the old woman search for the brush to get my hairs off their clothes.

September 11

There are some local elections going on. Someone died and now they have to replace him. We have had lots of leaflets come through the letterbox, each urging the old man and the old woman to vote for this person or that person.

Mostly they go straight into the bin with the old man shouting, 'Moron!' at each one.

I couldn't summon up any interest until I realised there wasn't one party representing cats. Disgraceful.

I've been up all night drafting my manifesto. Here's a brief resume of my manifesto:

1. An unlimited supply of cardboard boxes.

2. All furniture to be designated as scratching posts.

3. Free run of the house for sleeping spots - including on people's heads, on their laptops, in the middle of the bed while people are in it, on the top of the expensive ornaments on the top shelf.

4. Feeding on demand of fresh meat, fish and/or prawns with several treats thrown in at regular intervals.

5. Compulsory stroking by hoomans for at least two hours a day.

I was considering adding 'Home Rule for cats' - but we already have that.

It shouldn't be long before I'm Purrime Minister. Purrime. Geddit? Jeez, I'm good.

September 12

The old woman has bought a load of low calorie ready meals. She doesn't seem to realise that eating two at a time doubles the calories.

No grasp of basic maths, that's her trouble.

September 13

Today the old woman was toiling over a sketch pad, mapping out a floral blueprint for the garden. For the spring she envisaged a plot covered by swathes of brightly-coloured daffodils, narcissi, tulips and lily-of-the-valley. The old man and the old woman then spent all morning planting spring-flowering bulbs.

I spent all afternoon digging them up again.

Look, in my defence I thought I was being helpful. To my aesthetic sensibilities there were far too many bulbs. They needed thinning out and I was the one to do it. I can't deny I took some kind of pleasure from the task. It was very satisfying getting my paws dirty, digging down, searching around and then hooking out the little bulb.

I was tidy. After playing with the bulbs, throwing them up in the air and pouncing on them, I lined them up neatly outside the back door.

My task done, I padded across the kitchen floor, into the sitting-room and up onto the sofa, leaving clumps of rich red earth as I went.

The old woman arrived home from work, humming brightly. She dumped her work paraphernalia in the hall and flung open the sitting-room door. Her mouth fell open.

'Toffee!' she yelled. 'What have you been doing?' Her eyes followed the trail of mud from door to sofa. Tutting, she went to fetch cleaning products.

I heard a sharp scream. 'Noooooooo!'

There's a saying, isn't there, 'discretion is the better part of valour', which, to paraphrase means 'get the hell out of there before you get your arse whipped'. I took off for my hidey hole under the shed where I stayed for a couple of hours cleaning off my paws and snoozing. I waited long enough for the old man and the old woman to get worried about me. It started to get dark and I heard them calling.

I tentatively approached the old man and wound myself around his legs. He picked me up.

'There you are. You're a very naughty girl, aren't you?' But his voice was soft, not angry.

The old woman sighed and tickled me under the chin.

September 14

Just after breakfast I spotted two chicken breasts on the kitchen counter. They looked lonely so I carried them into the garden and hid them under the wheelbarrow.

Hasta la vista, baby. I'll be back.

September 15

DO. NOT. TALK. TO. ME.

RAJAH/PERCY. STOLE. MY. CHICKEN.

(Which I had been saving for a rainy day. Today was raining.)

September 16

I wish the old man and the old woman weren't such restless sleepers. They throw their arms about, call out and twitch. How am I supposed to get any sleep on your head?

September 17

Mmm, I hear a new garden pest is on the menu. Personally, I think all living things in the garden are lunch or recreation.

I am on the lookout for something called Rosemary Beetle. I was on the old woman's lap as she read in the newspaper about this beetle thing which is partial to herbs, especially rosemary, hence the name.

Now I'm keeping an eye on the herb garden (herb garden being a rather grand term for one straggly rosemary bush, some half-dead sage, a sprig or two of thyme and some mint in a broken pot) and if I spot Rosemary, she'll be toast.

I stared at that herb garden for hours and not a glimpse of a pest of any kind.

Rosemary Beetle? FAKE NEWS.

September 18

Oh yeah, blame me, old woman, as per usual. Why do you always assume I'm up to no good? Life is so UNFAIR. I'm being purrsecuted. Now, where did I hide that bacon?

Hungry.

September 19

I fancied a bit of a scratch in my abdominal area but both the old man and the old woman ignored me as I assumed the position. They were dashing about doing what hoomans do (lots of dashing, not much achieved).

So I put my exclusive Tummy Tickle plan into action. I threw myself in front of the old man's feet and rolled onto my back. Not too close, I didn't want him to step on me with his huge size 10s.

What this position says is, 'Look at me, I trust you so much that I am baring my stomach to you. Is it too much to ask for a rub in exchange for my undying love?'

He smiled down at me, picked me up and started to rub my tummy. Unfortunately, he rubbed it for a millisecond too long and I sunk my teeth into his hand, but the principle holds.

Read and learn, kittens. Read and learn.

September 20

The old man seems to think I sleep too much. I do not. I have to sleep to conserve my energy for when I have to leap into action. Like when…um…like when…um. It'll come to me after I've had a nap.

September 21

After a busy day the old man and the old woman opted for an early night. I crept in about half an hour later and they were both fast asleep. I thought I'd give them sweet dreams so I settled down between them and started to sing a lullaby. Were they grateful? No, they were not.

They awoke. 'For goodness sake, Toffee,' the old man said sleepily. 'Why all the racket?'

The old woman sat bolt upright and switched on the light. 'Whassup?' she shouted, like some bad-tempered teenager teleported from the 1980s.

'It's only Toffee,' said the old man. 'She's having a funny five minutes.' He began to stroke me and said, 'Settle down, girl. Time to sleep.'

The old woman switched out the light and sighed deeply.

'That cat is absolutely nuts,' she said.

Charming.

September 22

The old woman is away until tomorrow helping niece Violet with a baby-related problem. Don't know why they don't trade Little Person in for a cat. It's very ugly and very grabby, not nearly as attractive as a certain charming ginger girl I could mention. Just saying.

While she's away the old man is attempting some DIY, putting up new shelves in the utility room. He has a big box of tools and is wearing a tool belt. I sit and watch him from the laundry basket. 'Here's some good advice for you, Toffee,' he says. 'Measure twice and cut once.'

Or, as it turned out, measure twice, cut several times, swear a lot.

He's usually good at this kind of thing but the six-pack of beer he consumed may have clouded his judgement a smidgeon.

He spent the evening watching the tellybox, eating a takeaway, belching, farting and scratching himself.

In the meantime, the fridge has been declared an official biohazard.

I'll be glad when the old woman gets home and civilisation returns.

September 23

The old woman came home and surveyed the handiwork in the utility room. She frowned quite a lot at the uneven shelves and rough edges.

'I thought you were supposed to be good at DIY,' she said. 'Hasn't anyone ever told you that you should measure twice and cut once?'

The old man got a bit huffy at this slur on his manhood and a row ensued. It finished when he stalked out of the room saying, 'It's a good job I married Miss Right. Pity I didn't know it was Miss ALWAYS Right.'

September 24

The old man went to a friend's house for a boys' night out to watch two grown men in baggy shorts and tasteless tattoos batter each other to within an inch of their lives - boxing I think they call it. He set off down the road with a few cans of beer clanking around in his supermarket carrier bag looking more like a wino than a sports aficionado.

The old woman and I cuddled up on the sofa while she groomed me and rubbed my ears. She ate chocolates and I had a few juicy prawns.

I think a good time was had by all - he rolled in quite late minus the beer at any rate. He hadn't had too much to drink because he could remember that the British boxer in typical Brit-style had put up a plucky fight before losing to the Russian.

There's a surprise.

September 25

I don't know why everyone thinks dogs are so bloody intelligent. What's clever about doing stupid tricks? A performing seal can do tricks.

September 26

The old man and the old woman were on their laptops. I'm a bit pissed off with them to tell you the truth as neither would allow me to sit on their keyboards. I was only trying to be helpful, keeping a look out for viruses. I'm sure if I spotted one I could kill it with one swipe.

The old woman said: 'Look at this, Interesting Facts About A Cat's Nose.' I went cross-eyed trying to look at my own nose. It didn't seem 'interesting' to me. The old man looked up briefly from an 'interesting' (oh yeah?) website of woodworking machinery.

The old woman started to read: 'A cat's nose plays a crucial role in their lives, trapping bacteria and other nasty irritants found in the air.'

Enough! I don't even want to THINK about bacteria on the end of my nose, thank you very much.

She read on and on and on. It was an interesting article but her voice is a bit 'blah'. I could tell the old man had stopped listening. He was gazing lovingly at a state-of-the-art spindle moulder. (Yes - there IS such a thing.)

I was concentrating, not on the article but on trying to extricate a particularly sticky burr from my behind but I heard this bit: 'A cat's sense of smell is also often referred to as 'olifaction' and it's much keener than that of a hooman.' So, olifaction guaranteed - LOL, I'm so funny...

Then it all got a bit icky. The old woman rabbited on about discharges, fungal infections and abscesses. Just stop now.

She listed some more 'interesting' facts but they were all wasted on me because I already nose all about it. Nose. Get it?

My comedic talents are wasted living in this house.

September 27
I have burned my bum.
Who burns candles while having a bath anyway?
The old woman, that's who.

September 28
I occasionally feel the need to pass on my expertise to younger cats, many of whom seem not to know how to behave in certain situations.

Today my subject is doors.

You are young and at your stage of life probably think doors are only ever opened by your pet hooman. But there will come a time when you will need to attract their attention because they are so dim they don't realise you need to come in or go out. So one of the first skills you need to learn is how to get your pet hooman to open the door on command.

After all, you don't want to lose your dignity and get stuck half in and half out, do you?

Often all that is required is sitting in front of the door and meowing in your most annoying tone of voice. The times I've heard the words, 'For goodness sake, Toffee, stop that caterwauling and go outside if you're going to make that racket,' before the door is flung open.

Sometimes your pet hooman is on the opposite side of the door in a room you want to enter. The 'annoying meow' tactic may work here too. Sometimes, though, they pretend they can't hear you. In which case you have to proceed to Stage Two. Start scratching the door. For some reason pet hoomans hate this and will rush to open the door before you have done more than make a few marks on it.

Other useful tactics include jumping up at the door handle, rubbing your hind feet on the floor as if you need a 'comfort break' and sitting an inch from the door and glaring at it.

If the worst comes to the worst and your pet hoomans are so terminally stupid they don't understand what you want (or if you are home alone), you can always open the door yourself. This is tricky and will require practice but it's not impossible. Leap onto the handle and cling on for dear life. It should turn downwards and the door swing open.

Now pay attention, class. This last module is the most important part of my lesson plan.

If your pet hooman has gone to a lot of trouble to open the door for you - maybe they were in the middle of a phone call, busy doing chores or engrossed in a tellybox show - it is imperative that as soon as the door is open you turn around and go back into the room. You can, if you wish, stand or sit in the open doorway and stare out for quite considerable time while they wait (usually impatiently). However, the end result is the same. You end up back where you started from.

September 29

TODAY WAS ONE OF THE WORST DAYS IN MY LIFE.

The old man and the old woman look like a normal friendly couple. They look after me. They pet me. They smile at me. So this morning when the old man picked me up for a cuddle, I thought nothing of it.

But then they struck, like a pair of evil cat kidnappers. The old man trapped me by wrapping a towel around me. The old woman approached with an evil look in her eye and a small white round thing in her hand.

'Come on, Toffee, open up. It's just a little pill,' she cooed. But she didn't fool me. I struggled violently to escape the clutches of Towel. I shredded Towel and also man's hand. He yelled and dropped me. I tried to escape but Towel had me by the legs. The old woman leapt on me and wrestled me to the sofa. 'Quick, quick!' she shouted to the old man. He leapt forward, prised open my mouth and pushed horrible white round thing down my throat.

I gagged and threw up white round thing plus my dinner all over the old woman's blouse. She ran off to the bathroom shouting, 'Ew, ew, ew!' I extricated myself from Towel and ran as fast as I could out through the cat flap and up the nearest tree where I stayed for the rest of the day, ignoring the old man and the old woman's blandishments to come down.

When I came in later, the old man and the old woman's were looking very shame-faced - as well they might. They had put lovely fresh prawns in my bowl so I have NEARLY forgiven them. I enjoyed the prawns even though they had a slight bitter taste. But I persevered. I do love prawns.

The old man and the old woman's smiled knowingly at each other.

'I think next time we won't try to administer the worming tablet orally,' said the old man as he clutched his lacerated hand.

'No, I think via food is the better option,' said the old woman.

Not a clue what they're talking about.

September 30

The old woman has come home from Big Bargains with five boxes of my favourite cat food, each containing 40 pouches. I've decided they're no longer my favourite.

OCTOBER

October 1

The old man has another cold. He calls it flu. The old woman calls it Man Flu and is less than sympathetic.

Today he came home after a visit to the chemist's with sachets of Lemsip, cough medicine, sore throat pastilles, sinus spray and a box that I will have to investigate later. He's in the sitting-room with the fire on. It stinks in there - what with his medicinal remedies and his sweating.

I'm keeping well out of it. I don't want to catch something the old woman calls Hypochondria - sounds nasty to me.

I have investigated the box the old man brought home from the chemist. I think it was a toy he forgot to give me in his flu-addled state. I had great fun pulling out its papery contents, shredding them and scattering them all over the house.

He came downstairs, sniffing and coughing, and then shouted: 'Toffee, what have you done with my dissues, you liddle modster! How am I dowing to blow my dose!'

What's he saying? Something about Lidl. Hope he's going there to buy prawns.

October 2

I think the old man is feeling slightly better. He's still in his dressing-gown and pyjamas but he managed to make himself sausage, eggs and chips and pour himself a glass of beer while the old woman was at work.

He saw me staring at the beer. 'It's vital to keep my fluid levels up,' he said. Humph.

He retired to the sitting-room where he watched the telly-box and laughed fit to bust at some young men playing pranks on each other. He later made a cup of coffee and snaffled half a packet of chocolate digestive biscuits.

He must be getting his energy back because he put on some music. He worked up quite a sweat practising his best dance moves, which involved much hip thrusting and arm waving. When we heard the front door slam, he leapt back onto the sofa and turned the music right down.

The old woman came into the sitting-room and said: 'How are you feeling?'

He whimpered: 'Not too bad. I'm feeling a *little* better.'

She pressed the back of her hand to his forehead.

'God, you're really hot!' she said. 'You'd better rest for a little while longer.'

The whimpering continued: 'If you say so, dear.'

Shameless.

October 3

The old man is still at home getting under my paws all day but I can tell he's getting bored. He's been flopping about in his pyjamas playing video games, watching the tellybox, falling asleep and eating and drinking too much.

The old woman's brief bout of compassion is waning rapidly.

She marched into the sitting-room tonight and started gathering up dirty dishes and empty cold-sachet papers.

'You're not so ill that you can't at least clear up after yourself,' she said.

'But I'm poorly!' he shouted after her retreating behind.

She kicked the sitting-room door shut with a bang as she left.

I was trapped with the old man who grimaced at me.

'Some people have no sympathy,' he muttered.

Good job he can't read my mind.

October 4

Thank goodness. The old man has dragged himself back to work today and I have the house to myself. What to do to fill my busy day. Think I'll start with a relaxing nap.

October 5

I was investigating a small scab on my tail. I tried to grab it to have a closer look but my tail flopped just out of reach. You would think it had a mind of its own. I flipped around to try to get at it from another angle but it flopped again. Flip. Flop. Flip. Flop.

I heard a voice from the sitting-room door.

'What the hell are you doing, Toffee?'

The old man must have been watching my exertions. I ignored him, pounced and finally managed to capture my tail. I started chewing at the scab.

'Good Lord, Toffee, what a funny little weirdo you are.'

Weirdo?

This from the man who plucks his nose hairs with his wife's eyebrow tweezers and sings into his hairbrush with his collar up pretending to be Elvis.

October 6

The old man is considering buying a paper shredder. Why? He's already got one.

ME!

October 7

After watching a Youtube video last night about homemade gourmet cat food, The old woman decided to get busy in the kitchen and rustle me up something called A Feast Fit For A Feline. Big mistake. Big, big mistake. The woman can hardly boil an egg so what made her think she could rustle up fish pate, sushi balls and something she called pulled duck. Pulled? Where are they pulling it, back to the pond?

She didn't have a recipe and she couldn't find the Youtube video. 'I'll wing it, Toffee,' she said to me as I sighed and shook my head.

She spent ages staring at a fish. He stared right back with a pair of glassy eyes. Then she began to chop. Never in my life have I seen such carnage - and I am someone who butchers tiny creatures on a regular basis.

'Who'd have thought fish had so many bones?' she said. Yes,

who'd a thought…? I put my paw over my eyes.

She began to boil the fish and a vile smell crept over the kitchen, like a cross between week-old prawns, damp towels and smelly socks. She went a bit green and opened the back door as wide as it would go.

'Bet you love the smell, don't you, Toffee?'

I rolled over onto my back with my four legs rigid in the air.

'Oh, very funny, Toffee.'

Then she attacked the poor old duck. I don't know what he'd ever done to her but she was certainly getting her own back. She battered a fillet with a rolling pin - and seemed to enjoy it a bit too much, if you ask me.

'It has to be cooked long and slow,' she said, 'so that it's nice and tender and can be pulled with a fork.' Into the oven went Donald.

While he was tenderising, she set about making sushi balls. She rolled up the chopped poached fish. The ball fell apart. She rolled it up again. It fell apart again.

'Mmm, I can't really use a binding agent as you shouldn't eat things like flour, Toffee. I might just keep it as it is.' The fish sat in the dish, pale and collapsed, smelling even worse than it did in the saucepan if that were possible.

She began to chop it up into very fine pieces.

'I will very lightly cook this, Toffee, as I'm not sure whether I should give you raw fish. It would probably be all right but I don't want you to get worms.' I shuddered.

She popped the bowl into the microwave. Distracted by the smell of burning duck, she forgot about the microwaving fish. After five minutes the microwave went 'ding' and she pulled out a dish of rubber pellets.

The blackened duck was in no mood to be pulled anywhere so she abandoned that idea too.

So there on the kitchen counter were three dishes, one of smelly fish, one of rubberised fish and one of cremated duck. Aren't I the lucky one?

She set about cleaning up the kitchen as it all cooled.

The old man came home and inspected her afternoon's work. He glanced in my direction. I looked at him with imploring eyes.

He turned to the old woman. 'Why don't you go and have a rest while I feed Toffee?'

When she left the room, he swept the assorted animal remains into the bin and opened up a pouch of rabbit in gravy.

'There you are, girl. It'll be our secret.'

I love that man sometimes.

October 8

Today I caught my own breakfast and brought it indoors to finish it off in the warm. The old man and the old woman walked in on me as I chewed on an ex-mouse.

'Oh Lord, Toffee, you're such a monster!' said the old woman.

Offended, I looked up, briefly, but decided to let it go as I was enjoying my food. The old man laughed and put on this creepy voice.

'I ate his liver with some fava beans and a nice chianti,' he said.

What's he on about? I don't even like beans or chianti. The old woman turned on her heel and walked out.

'That's not funny. And you can clear up the mess when she's finished.'

The old man stopped laughing.

October 9

Why don't they make cat food out of mice?

October 10

'I love you,' said the old man.

'Oh, darling, I love you too,' said the old woman.

'I wasn't talking to you, I was talking to Toffee,' he said absentmindedly.

She is not best pleased and the old man is blethering about loving her too but she won't be placated.

October 11

I have a job. I have decided to become a self-employed inventor.

It all started when I was warming my behind on the old woman's laptop keyboard. She rushed towards me like an overweight whirling dervish and scooped me up.

'For goodness sake, Toffee,' she yelled. 'Look what you've done!'

There was pinging. In place of some neat typing there were lots of symbols. A light was flashing.

She lunged for the laptop and began tapping keys as if her life depended on it.

'Control Z, control Z, control Z,' she kept muttering before slumping back in her chair and glaring at me.

Look, old woman. If you don't want me to lie on something then don't make it warm.

The whole incident got me thinking. Later today I'm going to invent a cat basket in the shape of a large laptop, complete with keys. It will be heated electrically and will ping if you touch the C, A or T with your paw.

I'd buy it. Or rather, I'd wait until the Amazon site was open and then walk up and down the keyboard in the hope that I'd ordered it.

October 12

The inventing is going well. I am in the concept stage for my laptop cat basket. Now I have turned my attention to another nifty idea.

Fellow cats, you know how annoying it is when your hoomans are out and you awake from a nap and have to get up and walk all the way to your food bowl. How much nicer would it be to stay in your comfy chair and have the food come to you.

You can have remote-controlled cars so why not remote-controlled food bowls? Press a button and wheels descend from the container. It rolls across the floor and makes its way to wherever you are sitting.

If you are upstairs, press another button and propellers come into play, flying your meaty chunks straight to your resting place.

I'm a genius.

October 13

The old woman was telling the old man about a work colleague who had got rid of her cat after moving in with a man whose kid was allergic to them. Should have got rid of the kid.

Just my opinion.

October 14

The old woman returned from shopping very happy.

'Look what I've got for Toffee,' she said excitedly to the old man.

He groaned.

'What's that supposed to mean?' she asked, annoyed.

'Remember the cat harness [dear God, no] and the Christmas jumper [I shuddered] and the wind-up mouse [buried in the garden]?'

'But she's really going to love this,' said the old woman. 'It's a laser.'

I was on the sofa. I looked up at the pair of them. Laser. No idea what Laser is and unless it's edible and tastes of prawns, I don't want to know.

The old woman spent about half an hour trying to remove Laser from the plastic wrap and another half an hour putting in a fiddly little battery. I watched. The old man smiled.

Then she switched it on and shone a bright dot at me.

Is this Laser? I put out a paw to touch it.

'There, see!' said the old woman. 'She's playing with it!'

She moved the dot slowly across the room. I watched it. I stretched. She moved it back in front of me and then moved it away again. I stared and yawned.

'Oh yes,' said the old man. 'I can see that's going to provide hours of fun.'

'She's not used to it yet, is she?'

She kept moving this dot around the room while the old man sat in the chair, his arms folded.

'You're putting her off,' the old woman grumbled.

I closed my eyes. By the time I opened them again the old man and the old woman had gone to bed.

The next day I spotted Laser in the wastepaper bin. Best place for it.

October 15

The old man had a busy day at work.

'It's a dog eat dog world,' he said.

YAY!

October 16

I'm going for a siesta. Wake me at teatime and not a second before.

October 17

I ate a huge bowl of salmon in jelly followed by another bowl of milk. I then dragged myself to the sitting-room and flopped down on the sofa, occasionally licking my distended stomach.

The old man rubbed my head. 'Toffee's on the python diet,' he said to the old woman. 'She swallows a pig whole and then doesn't eat for a year.'

A year? I think 30 minutes should do it.

October 18

YOUR bed? I don't think so, buster.

October 19

I had a busy day, what with guarding my territory from intruders and becoming a big game hunter (mouse was rather large). So I slept all evening stretched out with my head on the old woman's lap and my arse on the old man's leg.

'Toffee makes a sloth look like a cheetah on speed,' said the old man.

What's a sloth? Must be something pretty damn fast.

October 20

The old woman sprayed around some cheap air freshener she bought in Big Bargains.

The old man walked in and said, 'God almighty. Toffee hasn't taken to peeing in the house, has she?'

Jeez. Why drag me into this?

October 21

Today I was in the dog house (What a stupid saying. I wanted to say 'cat house' but that doesn't mean the same thing at all). Anyway, I broke the old woman's best vase in a chasing a spider along a shelf incident.

My bad.

She's got that 'I'm so disappointed in you' face on. You know, the one that makes her look like she's chewing on a lemon - all pursed lips and scrunched up eyes. But I sat in front of her, looking cute as only I can, and reached out to touch her leg with my paw.

She melted, of course, picked me up and said for the umpteenth time: 'What am I going to do with you Toffee?' You'd think she'd know by now.

GIVE ME PRAWNS.

October 22

There's another cat in the house. She's ginger, like me, and looks beautiful and intelligent. Oh, hang on a minute.

Mirror.

October 23

The old woman has been shopping again. Today she came home with a pack of socks for the old man and some feathers on a stick for me. She's not one of the world's big spenders and had found these in the Pound Shop, which set the old man off.

'How much were the socks?'

'£1 - from the Pound Shop.'

'And how much was the toy?'

She sighed. '£1.'

'How much did you say the socks were?'

She glared at him. 'I know what you're doing and I'm not going to play your silly game.'

Half an hour later and my toy lay shredded on the carpet and the old man was trying to squeeze his fat feet into socks obviously a size too small.

The old man looked me and shook his head.

'A bargain, eh Toffee?' He swept up the remains of the toy to put in the bin and carried his socks upstairs to stow away in the drawer.

October 24

The old woman bought some new brand of dry cat food with added vitamins. She poured some into my bowl. I sniffed it but was not impressed. I tentatively took a nibble. It tasted like rancid dog poo and I spat it out. But she continued trying to encourage me to eat it.

'Come on, Toffee, it could add years to your life,' she said, waving a few nuggets in front of my nose.

She could be right. I feel years older already.

October 25

COD. COD. FRESH COD.

That. Is. All.

October 26

A strange hooman walked into the sitting-room. I gave her a quick sniff and realised it was the old woman. I was still dubious that it wasn't some stranger who, by a quirk of fate, happened to smell like her. Then this hooman bent down, rubbed my ears and said, 'Hello, Toffee.'

The old man strolled in and did a double-take.

'Oh my God, darling, you look, you look, you look, umm different!'

'I do, don't I? I've been to the department store and had a makeover on the beauty counter.'

Makeover? More like runover. She had an orange face with bright red lips, two jet black eyebrows crawling over her face like two slugs trying to effect an escape, and many shades of sludge green all around her eyes. Her eyelashes were twice as long as normal and were caked in something black.

I hope she's not running away to join the circus. I need her to feed me prawns.

The old man stared and then stared even harder when she plonked a big bag full of painty face things on the coffee table.

'How. Much?'

'You can't put a price on beauty,' she said as she swanned off to stare at herself in the mirror.

October 27

The old woman got up early and tried to replicate yesterday's face-painting. When she'd finished she looked like she did yesterday - only wonkier.

She got home from work in the evening and marched straight to the bathroom where she removed every bit of her morning's handiwork. She came back with a face like thunder and plonked herself down on the sofa.

The old man came home and asked her what was wrong.

'WRONG? What makes you think anything is WRONG!'

'Just a hunch...'

He then asked, 'Where's all your make-up gone?' Her face went as red as this morning's lips.

'WHY? WHY, did you let me go out like that?'

'But, but, you looked ... very nice,' he lied, not too convincingly.

'Well, no one else seemed to think so. They SNIGGERED at work. I could hear them. Sniggering and whispering. Then on the bus on the way home a man asked me how much I charged. He thought I was a HOOKER.'

I have no idea what a hooker is but it's obviously something not very nice.

The old man opened his mouth to utter some witty remark but caught a glimpse of her face and realised she was genuinely upset. He put his arm around her.

'You always look beautiful to me,' he said. 'You are the most beautiful woman in the world, with or without make-up. Isn't she Toffee?'

I jumped up on to the sofa and put my paw on her arm.

She sniffed a couple of times, rubbed my ears and gave the old man a kiss.

'Well, whatever. I've learned my lesson. Less is more. Now let's get some tea.'

October 28

Of course I'm hugging you because I love you.

Also, feed me. Preferably prawns.

October 29

I am appalled by the behaviour of the old man and old woman. They went out last night and I didn't get my late night snack until 12.45 this morning. I'm thinking of imposing a curfew.

October 30

Excuse me for a moment. I'm working hard chewing this newspaper into thousands of tiny pieces and scattering them all over the house.

Exhausted.

October 31

It's Halloween so I've been stalking around the house and suddenly stopping and staring at corners as if there's something there. It's freaking out the old woman.

I ran through the house at a rate of knots as if followed by the hounds of hell. Then while the old woman was eating her lunch I stared into the distance and suddenly yowled.

Later as she was settling down to read a book I hid under behind the sofa. I waited until she was engrossed and then suddenly leapt out, clawing the air with my fur standing on end.

She let out a piercing scream.

I love Halloween.

Trick or treat!

NOVEMBER

November 1

The old man and the old woman were trying out a new brand of cat food on me.

'It's slightly dearer than your normal pouches,' the old woman told me. 'But if you like it, we don't mind paying the extra.'

They watched over me expectantly as I took a nibble.

I was getting mouse liver, a hint of wet rabbit skin. I was getting scent of woodlouse droppings. I was getting sick. Heave. Heave. Quick, quick.

The old woman flung open the back door as the old woman scooped me up and put me outside.

When I returned the new cat food had disappeared and the old brand was in the dish.

'I don't think we'll try that again,' said the old woman.

'Best not,' said the old man.

November 2

Caught a mouse.

Toffee 007. Licensed to kill.

November 3

I found out something interesting today. The old woman was reading one of her books about cats.

First of all she read out about how hoomans domesticated cats. She must have misread that bit. I think she meant to say, how cats domesticated hoomans. We cats saw we could make an easy life for ourselves if we protected stores of grain from rats and mice. Easy peasy. So we gradually tamed hoomans so they were docile enough to let us lie in front of their fires, in between bouts of hunting for our supper. Put a rat or a mouse up against our towering intellect and it's no contest. Eventually the Egyptians worshipped us - very clever people, those Egyptians.

Then the old woman's voice grew quiet and she glanced in my direction. I feigned sleep.

She whispered to the old man. 'Don't tell Toffee but in the Middle Ages cats came to be seen as demons and witches' familiars. They were persecuted and nearly wiped out.' I half opened one eye and saw that hers were full of tears. She's soppy sometimes, that woman.

Then came the GOOD NEWS. There were so few cats left that when rats carrying the Black Death arrived in Britain the disease was rampant. No clever cats to keep them under control, you see. Yay! Serves those stupid hoomans right. Or am I being a bit harsh?

So we cats came into our own again, especially when the Great Plague hit London. People could see how useful we were. Then in 1750 we were introduced into America to keep down the rodent population.

Now in the 21st Century, we are worshipped again.

Well, I am.

November 4

The old woman is in trouble. She was reading a Top Tips column in a magazine. One said that to cure smelly shoes, put a piece of toast in them over night. Unfortunately, she forgot to take the toast out in the morning.

I was awoken by the old man shouting, 'WHAT THE ...'

November 5

Tonight I sat by the old woman's laptop as she surfed the net. Lord, that woman doesn't half read and write a load of rubbish. She was on Facebook swapping inane comments with her equally dopey friends. She was 'liking' every post and picture and writing things like, 'We must meet up SOON, babe, it's been too long,' to people she would cross the street to avoid.

Then she started clicking through to videos after reading, 'You must watch this!!!! This video is taking the world by storm!!!!'

Dear website, I have news for you; no I mustn't and no it isn't.

November 6

Come rub my belly. Look at me so cute here lying on my back. You know you want to. Come on, get suckered in by the Belly Rub of Death.

ATTACK!

'For God's sake, Toffee, you really have no people skills at all, do you?' grumbled the old man while rubbing his hand.

Of course I have people skills. It's just that you dummkopfs and jugheads don't realise it.

November 7

I've been practising my death stare for when Rajah/Percy next infiltrates my garden. Eyes wide open? Eyes narrowed? Sideways glare? Full-on glower?

I realise the old man and the old woman have been watching me.

'What on earth goes on in that cat's head?' asked the old man.

'I often wonder but have decided that it's best not to know,' said the old woman.

You're not wrong there.

November 8

I have noticed over the last few months that my normally sleek, well-toned physique has become a little fluffy around the edges. I blame the old man and the old woman for allowing me too many treats like cheese and sausage off their plates.

In an effort to regain the body of a lean, mean fighting machine, I have taken up yoga.

There are many poses suitable for a fit young cat like me. I don't mind the Crane and the Cobra but I draw the line at the Downward Dog pose.

I have my standards.

November 9

Today I helped old man and the old woman with their paper-work. They had left the door to the office open with piles of papers on the desk. I went to investigate. It was obvious to someone with my analytical mind that the papers needed re-arranging into some kind of logical order.

I sniffed the first pile. It smelled papery. I sniffed a second pile. It smelled papery too. As did the third, fourth and fifth piles.

They obviously needed filing together under Smells Papery. So I knocked them all to the floor, where they lay in one big heap.

You're welcome.

November 10

I sat on the old woman's knee, purring.

'Have you noticed how Toffee has several different purrs?' said the old woman. 'Sometimes they're deep, sometimes higher, sometimes slow and sometimes fast.'

'Oh yes,' said the old man, 'She has several purrmutations,' and laughed like he'd said something clever.

Dunderhead.

November 11

Today I have been musing on the existential question, if the old woman neglects to fill my bowl to the very top, is it seven-eighths full or one-eighth empty?

This question has been occupying my brain since this morning when I heard the sound of doors slamming and pouches being ripped open. About time, I thought, breakfast!

I ran into the kitchen and slid to a halt beside my bowl.

Umph. The bowl was only seven-eighths full. The old woman was standing over my food bowl, pouch in hand. I meowed loudly and looked at my bowl. My eyes said: 'I'm eating noth-ing until you have fulfilled your obligations as a member of my staff.'

The old woman stared back. I stared at her. I looked at my bowl again. She shook her head. I sat on my haunches and looked accusingly up at her. I meowed loudly again. She continued shaking her head. I meowed louder.

Then she said: 'Oh for goodness sake, Toffee,' and retrieved another pouch of food.

My original instincts were correct.

The bowl was one-eighth empty.

November 12

The old man told me if I keep scratching the furniture he's going to give some of my innards to his violinist friends.

He'll have to catch me first.

November 13

I don't care if you are in the middle of clearing out that cupboard, I want petting NOW.

Can't get the staff.

November 14

I think I want some Depression. I'm not sure what Depression is but the old woman says her friend has it and it makes her want to stay in bed all day. That sounds good to me. I shall have to investigate further to see exactly what Depression contains - I'm hoping prawns.

November 15

The news was on the tellybox and they flashed up a picture of a big ginger cat, nearly as stunning as me. I pricked up my ears. Chester the cat may have been nearly as handsome as me but not half so clever.

He had knocked over a bottle of beer, its contents spilling into his food bowl. The stupid animal drank it and then staggered outside and picked a fight with two delivery men who were baring their scratches for the camera.

Chester then staggered back home and passed out half way through the cat flap.

The old woman looked at the old man.

'Now I believe in reincarnation,' she said. 'Your father has come back to life as Chester!'

The old man gave a wry smile. 'Oh, very bloody funny.'

November 16

I am sad to report it is getting more obvious every day that the old man and the old woman are getting past it. They are galloping full pelt towards senility, which is worrying. For me.

The first thing I noticed was that the hearing was going. They both ignored me as I meowed, and meowed, and meowed, and meowed, and meowed, and meowed while they were eating their prawn salads. Would it have killed them to have thrown one or two in my direction? Not only deaf - but, I hate to say it - tending on the cruel side.

Now the eyesight is becoming a problem. Yesterday The old man picked me up - as I allow him to from time to time - UPSIDE DOWN. The indignity. My arse was in his face and my head was on that huge round thing he calls a stomach. Then he dropped me. Good job I have the reflexes of a well-honed athlete or there could have been a nasty accident.

I am now afraid to sleep on their faces when they are in bed in case they stop breathing altogether.

Then the other night the old man flexed his hands, winced, and said he was afraid Arthur Itis was coming. The old woman looked concerned and said, 'It's a sign of old age.'

Who is this Arthur Itis? Is he coming to take the old man away to The Home for the Terminally Bewildered?

I know I complain about the pair of them but I wouldn't to be without them. I have got used to their funny little ways and I have spent years training them. I really don't want to start from scratch with another couple.

November 17

I tried to lend a paw while the old woman was changing the duvet. I tried to help her pull off the cover. She put me on the floor. I tried to help her remove the pillowcases. She put me on the floor. I tried to smooth out the bottom sheet by running all over it. She put me on the floor. I tried to test the softness of the duvet as she was straightening it out. She put me on the floor.

Jeez. There's no helping some people.

November 18

The old woman was reading the old man his horoscope. It said that today he would have the energy to gets lots done.

He laughed. 'Does Toffee's say today she will eat, sleep and run around like a fool?'

He's a muttonhead.

November 19

This morning I woke the old man and the old woman at 6am, demanding my breakfast. Later I dragged my toys all around the sitting-room. The old woman stood on one and then tidied them all away. I meaningfully stared at the cushion on the sofa until she plumped it up for me to lie on.

She sighed and said, 'Toffee, you treat this house like a hotel.'

Yes, well, you two better shape up or you'll be getting a crap review on TripAdvisor.

November 20

I have found yet another thing that the old man and the old woman do not like. They dislike being awoken at 4am by a mouse running over the duvet. Don't know why. I thought it was a good present that showed my appreciation of the fresh prawns they gave me for tea yesterday.

Seems not. There was initially much shouting and then much running about with a plastic container and a piece of cardboard. They eventually trapped the mouse under the container and slid the cardboard underneath. Then - you'll find this hard to believe - they let the mouse go in the garden. There was zero attempt to play with it or leap on it or eviscerate it.

Weird.

November 21

Why won't you let me sit on your lap while you're on the toilet?

Feeling rejected.

November 22

Today I saved the old man and the old woman from certain death. While they were out shopping, a killer landed in the garden. It came blowing in through the trees, skittered across the lawn and came to rest on a rosebush. It was wearing what I assume was a T-shirt with the words *Tesco. Every Little Helps* on it. It blew in the wind making a roaring noise.

I attacked and tore that monster to shreds. When the old woman came home she removed pieces of him which were wound around my paws. And all she said was: 'Where did you get that carrier bag, Toffee?' So, even though at great personal risk I got rid of the Carrier Bag Monster, did they thank me? No they did not.

Some people are so ungrateful.

November 23

I'm sitting here with my paws over my ears. The old man and the old woman are having an almighty humdinger. The row started about whose turn it was to sort the recycling. I suppose I haven't helped by scattering and shredding a pile of newspapers all over the utility room.

The ruckus has now escalated and the old woman is shouting about something that happened in 2008. The old man is shouting back about how she has the memory of an elephant.

'Are you calling me an elephant?'

'If the cap fits...'

'You pig!'

'You elephant!'

Indoor voices please, you two. Indoor voices.

November 24

The old man and the old woman were stuck in traffic and came home late from work. They dashed about doing chores and cooking tea. The old woman looked at me curled up on the sofa. 'It's all right for you, Toffee, you don't have a job.'

Don't have a job? I'm a food critic, food inspector, quality controller, security guard, cardboard box inspector, model and masseur, to mention but a few.

Don't tell me I don't have a job, lady.

November 25

'Look how sweet Mrs Hartley's grandchildren are, out playing in the garden,' said the old woman.

Children? I thought they were garden gnomes.

November 26

In a flagrant miscarriage of justice, I have been jailed. There I was minding my own business investigating a spider under the bed when the door slammed. I have scratched it, meowed at it and jumped at it but it refuses to open.

You dirty rats, you've locked me in the slammer and it's a hell hole. There's nothing here to rest on but a thick duvet on a king size bed. But I must try to sleep to conserve my strength.

Five minutes in and I've forgotten what it's like to be free - to feel the wind in my fur and be in the warm embrace of Mr Fluffy Bum

It's been at least ten minutes. Feeling woozy through lack of food.

A quarter of an hour and still no sign of my captors.

Twenty minutes in and I find a spider - now an ex-spider.

Twenty-five minutes in the clink and I'm starting to feel uncomfortable. Nothing resembling a litterbox in this hell on earth.

Half an hour, and I hear footsteps on the stairs. I once more meow and scratch at the door.

It opens!

'Sorry, sweetie, I didn't realise I'd shut you in,' says the old woman with an armful of clean bedding.

I dash through her legs.

Out of my way, woman. Need a wee, need a wee, need a wee, need a wee, need a wee.

November 27

The old man and the old woman are stalking the sitting-room.

'What IS that smell?' the old man asks as they search every-where.

'It's vile,' says the old woman, 'Like something's died in here.'

They turn over cushions and look under chairs. Finally they

find something behind the bureau.

So that's where I put that lump of cod. I've been searching high and low for it for a week now.

Where are you putting it? Bring it back! It's mine, I tells ya, ALL MINE.

November 28

I have appointed myself official food taster.

The old woman caught me testing her spaghetti bolognese by licking the pasta and sampling the meat sauce.

She said: 'Ew, for goodness sake, Toffee,' and dumped it in the bin.

Just as well. It needed more seasoning.

November 29

The old woman was telling the old man about a book she'd seen about testing your cat's IQ.

'It costs £10.99,' she said.

He stared at her. 'If you spend £10.99 on a book about a cat's IQ, then Toffee is more intelligent than you.'

Good job she hasn't bought that book. If she had, she would have flung it at the old man's head.

November 30

The old woman was at her laptop reading out a list of what the hooman body is made of. Apparently, almost 99% of the mass of the hooman body is made up of six elements: oxygen, carbon, hydrogen, nitrogen, calcium, and phosphorus. About 0.85% is composed of another five elements: potassium, sulphur, sodium, chlorine, and magnesium.

The old man looked at me and said, 'I reckon Toffee is about 99% prawns,' and laughed like a drain.

Numbskull.

DECEMBER

December 1

The old man came home from work and said to the old woman, 'I see you're testing the fire alarm again.' Pause. 'Or cooking, as I like to call it,' and then fell about laughing.

I fear he will have to wait a very long time before he gets his dinner.

December 2

The old man and the old woman have been really busy lately, attending to family matters and working hard, so they have not lavished as much attention on me as they usually do.

When I adopted them I knew I would have to take the rough with the smooth. I could, if wanted, get up from the comfy bed, side-step the tuna chunks and exit through the cat flap to find pastures new. But I have invested so much time in training these two that I don't think I can be bothered starting from scratch with another pet*.

*slave

When I was a young cat-about-town I disappeared for a couple of days, I came back to find posters put up all over the area saying, 'Have you seen this cat?' I wouldn't have minded but the photo they used of me didn't even feature my best side. And, really, did they have to tell everybody that I had a small bald patch on my tummy? Totally humiliating. Honestly, you can't trust them to do anything right.

When the pets are in the house, I try not to leave them alone for too long as they are prone to bad behaviour, like drinking too much beer and wine, watching too much tellybox, reading books and talking on the phone for hours to their friends and family. I have to nip this mischief in the bud by crawling all over them, demanding attention and keeping them busy with things like removing half-chewed mice from under the sofa.

I also keep them busy by walking over the fresh laundry with muddy feet (see previous diary entries), hiding vital accessories like car keys and shedding hair over their furniture, clothes and pillows.

Despite all these measures, the pets still sometimes misbehave so I have to discipline them. Firm but fair, is my motto. One method is lie enticingly on the sofa and let them stroke me and then GRAB! While they are screaming, I say YOU. WILL. NEVER. GIVE. ME. CHEAP. OFFAL. CHUNKS. IN. JELLY. AGAIN.

A word to my fellow felines, these are tried and trusted methods to get you back on top spot as numero uno in their life.

December 3

Wondering. Why don't hoomans lick their own bums?

They have no conception of basic hygiene.

December 4

The old man and the old woman had a row about whose job is the most difficult. They'd both had stressful days. She had computer problems and had to work late and he had some woodwork-related glitch pertaining to the mismeasurement of an oak door.

'It's easy for you,' she said. 'You don't have to struggle with bloody technology that's ALWAYS going wrong.'

'Easy? You don't have to work with idiots who can't even measure properly. I didn't get where I am today without knowing how to use a bloody tape measure.'

'No,' she said. 'You got where you are today because woodwork was the only exam you passed at school.'

A bit cutting, I thought.

December 5

The old man and the old woman watched a tellybox programme about evolution this evening. Hoomans evolved from apes.

No surprise there.

I am a close relative to tigers, lions, jaguars, pumas, cheetahs – all those fierce and beautiful felines. No surprise there either.

'Dogs have evolved to be man's companion and helper,' said the presenter.

And no surprise there, the creeps.

The old man looked at me and said, 'Cats have evolved to be demanding, fussy and high maintenance,' and laughed.

I 'accidentally' knocked over his cup of tea.

No surprise there.

December 6

There's a minuscule speck of dust floating in my water bowl. I CAN'T DRINK THIS, PEOPLE, IT'S CONTAMINATED!

Jeez.

December 7

The old man got home late from the pub last night after imbibing more alcohol than the recommended Government guidelines. He slept in the spare room and stumbled out of bed this morning with a white face and red eyes.

The old woman is stomping around with her arms folded, grunting and glaring at anything that gets in her path i.e. the old man.

He looks like a schoolboy with the bellyache and she looks like a constipated platypus.

December 8

Morning, peeps. I'm feeling pretty good at the moment having just spooked the old man and the old woman. Ha, ha! It was their own fault. I was up bright and early and where were they? Under the duvet, snoring, the pair of them.

I wandered over to my bowl and, guess what, the darned thing was empty. Not a sniff of chicken, rabbit or whatever to be found. I stalked around a bit, thinking they'll be up any minute but, no, they stayed in bed, even after I ran all over them and meowed piteously.

So what's a girl to do?

I cleared my throat, sat between their two heads and yowled as loud as I could. They both sat bolt upright as I curled up into a ball, the picture of innocence.

'What the bloody hell...' said the old man.

'We'd better go and have a look,' said the old woman. 'It sounded like an animal in pain.'

They went out into the garden but all was quiet.

While you're up could you sling a few meaty chunks in my direction, please?

Well, I got my breakfast and I'm now curled up on the settee as the pair of them are still wondering what the noise could have been.

December 9

The old woman made little cupcakes for me today. She spent ages mashing up prawns, tuna and egg whites. Cooked them and then decorated them with a tiny bit of grated cheese and prawns.

I love that woman.

The old man told her she had far too much time on her hands.

He's a twerp.

December 10

I left the food in my bowl this morning and slowly made my way to the sofa.

'Poor Toffee, are you feeling poorly?' asked the old woman.

I stared at her, slowly blinking my big eyes.

'Stay there, sweetie, I'll get you some prawns.'

After I'd gobbled up the handful of prawns, I leapt to my feet and finished off my breakfast in the bowl.

The old woman glared at me, hands on hips. 'Toffee, you are the most devious, manipulative animal I have every met!'

Compliments this early in the day? Thank you!

December 11

I am sitting here with my paws over my ears – the old man is reading a newspaper and ranting. Why he couldn't be satisfied with a magazine called Lovely Little Pussycats or What To Buy

Your Beloved Cat, I don't know. The old woman and I had to suffer a rant of epic proportions.

A celebrity had made the mistake of wearing RIPPED JEANS. You would have thought that this designer statement would be way above the concerns of a blue collar boy brought up wearing short trousers and holey T-shirts. But no. The working class bit was germane to his whole rant.

'Ripped jeans? With all her money? I wore those when I was ten, not because I was an effing model [hardly ...] but because we didn't have any effing money for new jeans. Who do they think they're kidding? It's all "oo, look at me. I have so much money I can wear ripped jeans and everyone will know I paid an effing fortune for them". Fools!'

The old woman picked me up and I held on to her gratefully. 'Come on, Toffee, let's go and find you some meaty chunks.' We managed to escape, the rants reduced to a distant rumble in a faraway room.

December 12

Today a man delivered the old man and the old woman's new vacuum cleaner. It's a state-of-the-art bagless upright with a quiet motor. So much better than the last one which made enough noise to wake the dead and invariably sent me running out into the garden as if pursued by the hounds of hell.

It was a monstrous machine so, obviously, I treated it as a monster. And attacked it. It fell open and I leapt on its internal organs. Did you know that monsters' stomachs are full of dust and fluff? It went everywhere, all over the sitting-room floor, covering the furniture, books, ornaments and me. I sneezed so much I threw up. While trying to escape the monster's clutches I pulled the lead and the monster flew across the room and ended up wedged under the sofa.

The old man and the old woman took one look at the chaos and decided Monstrous Machine had had its day. They cleaned it up to give it away to niece Clementine, a student, who is moving into a (catless) flat.

The old woman tried out her new machine. It glided effortlessly across the room, picking up everything in its path. Until... Stop! Stop! That's my toy! Give it back!

She switched off the machine, pulled Fluffy Bum from its jaws and threw it in my direction.

'You're going to have to be careful about where you leave your toys from now on, Toffee' she said.

I picked up Fluffy Bum and carried him into the kitchen.

'Don't worry,' I whispered, 'New vacuum's days are numbered...'

December 13

I was sitting on the old woman's lap, contentedly purring. For reasons that escape me, she decided to purr too. She sounds like an old lion with a throat infection. I hope she's not suffering from galeanthropy. This is a rare mental condition where people thinks they are cats.

They wish.

December 14

I was feeling in a friendly mood this evening. Nothing to do with the old man and the old woman eating their dinner off lap trays in the sitting room. Really. Although if you want to give me a morsel of fish, I won't say no.

I was sharing my favours between the two of them and this started a conversation about which one of them I liked best. The conversation developed into a bit of a row.

'I know how to settle this,' said the old man. 'I'll stand at one end of the room and you stand at the other and we'll see who she goes to.'

They both started calling me and I looked at one and then the other. Then I made a dash for the fish.

No contest.

December 15

There I was ferreting around in a carrier bag. 'Oh look, Toffee's playing with the bag,' said the old woman. 'Isn't she cute!'

The old man smiled.

What is the matter with those two? I am not PLAYING, I am searching for hidden treats and cat toys.

The darned thing was empty.

As per usual.

December 16

Today I discovered that standing on the little blue-light button on the old woman's laptop turns it off. I walked across it every time she got up from the desk - to get a cup of tea, to get a biscuit, to have a pee, to phone a friend, to answer the phone to a friend, to brush her hair, to switch on the radio... (she has the attention span of a retarded gnat).

She is now convinced it is broken and she and the old man spent ages trying to 'mend' it. She's very pleased with him because it's now fine.

Until tomorrow... (cue evil laugh).

December 17

I was on guard duty. I spotted a wolf and I needed to protect the old man and the old woman from its ravening jaws. I sat by the open back door and scanned the garden with my gimlet eyes. He was hiding under a bush – obviously terrified of this avenging ginger ninja.

Make one move, buster, and you're cat food.

'Oh no,' said the old woman. 'Someone's dropped a raggedy old teddy bear into our garden.'

DON'T APPROACH, OLD WOMAN. DANGER! DANGER!

Too late, she's dumped it in the rubbish bin.

Is tea ready yet?

December 18

The old man and the old woman got home from work to find all the sofa cushions in a pile under the kitchen table. I put on my best innocent look.

The old man crouched down to look under the table. 'Mmm, what have we here?' he asks.

'I detect one muddy footprint in the corner of this cushion and a little cluster of ginger hairs on this one. Here's a small depression - about the size of a - let me think - a medium-sized cat. Oh, and what's this? Could it be a couple of stray cat treats?

'Do you know anything about this, Toffee?'

OK, Sherlock bloody Holmes, I get the message.

December 19

The old woman has walked out of the kitchen, slamming the door behind her. The old man is sitting at the kitchen table grinning.

It's nearly Christmas so the old woman has been dashing about all over the place buying presents that will probably end up in the bin before the end of the year and inexpertly wrapping them at the kitchen table. Honestly, I could do a better job – and I have no opposable thumbs.

She's somewhat frazzled and maintains the old man doesn't do enough to help.

Then began one of those 'who does the most' arguments.

The old woman said: 'You should walk a mile my shoes,' to which the old man replied, 'I will. Then I'll be a mile away from your nagging and have a free pair of shoes.'

Hence, door slam and stalking out.

I'm keeping out of it.

December 20

The old man was watching a programme about people and their sheds. These were not like our garden shed, a rickety structure full of half empty paint tins and rusty tools. These were outdoor rooms with designer interiors, games rooms for men who have never grown up and pretty pads for the woman who has everything.

Then someone used the phrase 'man cave' which set the old man off on one of his rants.

'Man cave? If you mean an effing shed, call it an effing shed. Oo, I've put my collection of 1980s Playboy magazines in my man cave.

'NO! You're a pervert with a shed!'

I've blocked up my ears.

December 21

The old woman has been buying Christmas presents and has left her credit card beside the laptop.

*Whistles nonchalantly.

I jumped up beside the laptop and positioned a paw over the keyboard. A hand swooped down and picked me up. Another hand swooped down and palmed the card.

'I'll have that, thank you very much, Toffee.'

Spoilsport. SERVES YOU RIGHT IF YOU DON'T GET A CHRISTMAS PRESENT.

I have my eye on a clockwork turkey that lays eggs full of top quality cat food. You would have liked that.

Your loss.

December 22

Just because I unexpectedly dropped onto your head after leaping from the windowsill, there's no need to scream like a banshee.

Jeez.

December 23

The old man and the old woman have done their big Christmas food shop. I didn't know a famine of epic proportions was imminent. We seem to have enough food for a small town with enough left over for a village.

I watched as they packed everything away. 'Thank God that's done,' said the old woman as she flopped down on to a chair. The old man put the kettle on. 'Time for a nice cup of tea,' he said.

But I had been watching as they stuffed item after item into groaning cupboards but hadn't spotted any meaty chunks, salmon pate or rabbit in jelly. I jumped onto the table and into the last bag.

Nothing.

I emerged and gave an angry meow. The old man and the old woman looked at each other, shouted, 'We've forgotten the cat food,' simultaneously, pulled on their coats and made a dash for the door.

This was an hour ago and now I'm sitting here in front of the door, tail swishing, waiting for the scatterbrained pair to return.

I am not best pleased.

December 24

I love Christmas. So many dangly ornaments to play with, so many decorations to knock off shelves and that tree in the corner sitting there waiting for me to destroy it.

I get PRESENTS. I love all the crunchy treats and toys. Some of the bigger presents are all beautifully wrapped so I can shred the paper and sit in the cardboard box they come in - while ignoring the actual present, obvs.

Anyway, I have a busy day of sleeping ahead of me so I am wide awake for tomorrow.

December 25

Christmas Day.

I have a stocking! I have a stocking! I have a stocking!

Let me have it, let me have it, let me have it NOW!

The old man and the old woman are smiling indulgently at my efforts to pull the stocking down from where it is anchored to the mantelpiece. At last a claw hooks into the wool. I tug and the whole thing comes tumbling down on top of me.

They laugh. Is it funny? I ask you. Is it really funny? Apparently it is, judging by the way these two buffoons are reacting. I then realise that the old man is capturing the whole debacle on his phone. Oh God, I'll be on Facebook before I've even unwrapped the first present.

December 26

Thank goodness Christmas Day is over. The old man and the old woman have been spoiling me so much with tasty titbits that I can't move off this cushion.

December 27

I'm in trouble again. It was one small leap on to the mantelpiece for me but one giant drop to the floor for the swan ornament – a hideous thing the old woman's mother gave her for

Christmas.

She had her sucked lemon face on again. I'm beginning to know that face rather well. She plucked me off the shelf - quite roughly, I thought - and talked to me in that 'this hurts me as much as it hurts you' voice.

'Two days, I've had that swan, Toffee. TWO DAYS! There's hardly an ornament left in this house thanks to you – you... you... WRECKING BALL you.'

I stalked off, tail held high, arse swaying from side to side, nose in the air - just to show her I didn't give a damn.

The old man met me at the door and bent down to stroke me. He smiled slyly and whispered: 'I hated that bloody thing.' Then said loudly: 'Oh no, not that lovely swan your mother gave you!'

By now the old woman was sweeping up the pieces with a dustpan and brush.

'Yes, darling, I'm afraid it was. I don't want to ban Toffee from the sitting-room but she's such a menace on that mantelpiece.'

The old man rubbed my ears.

'No, we can't do that. Let's just make sure there's nothing breakable on the mantelpiece.'

Just occasionally the male of the (hooman) species is so much more practical than the female.

December 28

Rajah/Percy was sitting in my garden, stroking his whiskers with a supercilious look on his stupid face. He thinks he sooo bloody handsome when in reality he looks like he fell out of the ugly tree and hit every damn branch on the way down.

I sprinted towards him, hissing, and he legged it back over the fence. Yeah, run, you coward. Your disappearing arse is all I ever want to see of you.

I da man.

December 29

The old man has been using the toiletries set his auntie gave him for Christmas. He smells like butterscotch covered in washing-up liquid.

December 30

We watched a documentary about my cousin the cheetah tonight. They said ol' Cheeto is the fastest animal on earth (up to 70mph).

Wrong.

The fastest animal on earth is a cow pushed out of an aeroplane (up to 200mph).

You're welcome.

December 31

After a year in my company I expect you're wondering where this most intelligent and gorgeous of cats came from. So let me tell you.

The LIFE STORY of Toffee Cat (or how I came to own the old man and the old woman).

Version One: I was born a queen among cats in a palace made of kippers and ham. As monarch of the kingdom, I was given the title Scourge of the Rodents and spent my days learning to stalk, pounce and kill, like the warrior Ninja I am.

I dined on salmon, prawns and fillet steak and slept in a four-poster bed on a velvet cushion. All other cats bowed before me, crying out, 'Oh Mighty One,' as I passed by.

I had three servants, one to comb my whiskers, one to sharpen my nails and one to warm the litter tray before I used it.

But one day, a cloud fell over Toffee's kingdom. The evil Rajah/Percy, that twit of a part-Siamese cat, put a spell on the palace by breathing over it with his disgustingly evil cat breath. The miasmic clouds floated through the rooms rendering all who breathed it in unconscious.

Only one cat remained awake on account of having a bad cold and hence a blocked nose, and that was my dutiful servant, The Lady of the Whiskers. She spirited me away to a far off land to live in safety in the home of the old man and the old woman from whence one day I will RISE AGAIN to reclaim my kingdom.

Version Two: The old man and the old woman visited the cat rehoming centre and came home with me.

Ya pays yer money and takes yer choice.

HAPPY NEW YEAR, EVERYONE!

I hope you have enjoyed reading about my thrilling, prawn-filled life. If you have, please take the time to give me A VERY GOOD REVIEW on Amazon.

You can keep in touch by following me on:

Facebook: www.facebook.com/pg/toffeekeenorleach/posts/

Twitter: https://twitter.com/SoToffee

Instagram: www.instagram.com/notsosweettoffee/

Not So Sweet Toffee by Toffee Keenor Leach

www.notsosweettoffee.com

Printed in Great Britain
by Amazon